KEY WEST ‹

A JACK MARSH ACTION THRILLER

MIKE PETTIT

Key West Smackdown

A Jack Marsh Key West Action Thriller

Chapter 1

The trade winds blowing out of the southeast carried the smell of rain and salt that tickled the nose and squinted the eye, leaving grit at the corner of the mouth. A big storm brewing down in the Caribbean was headed for the Florida Keys and was predicted to bring trouble with it. Key West sat dead-center in the bull's-eye— waiting. The old town had been without rain for over a month and coral dust coated everything under a white powdery film that you couldn't get away from unless you took a day trip up to Miami to escape. Most locals sucked it up and went on about their routines as usual, not because they didn't like Miami, but most had shit jobs where they needed to work to pay their bills. Life in the Keys had always been tough. The only people who ever made any big money were crooks who stayed one step ahead of the law. Key West was the end of the line for most of the twenty-five thousand full-time residents. Most were there because they were wanted by the law, were running or hiding from their wives or husbands up on the mainland, or just had no other place to go after a lifetime of getting their asses kicked. Oh sure there were good people there too, the original "Conchs," as they called themselves, who were the rich and elite, riding above the fray. Then there were the ones who had made a go of it off the backs of the losers in town, or the tourists with dollars who flocked there in giddy droves to soak up the rum and sun. You couldn't run any farther than Key West and still be in the U.S. Next stop ... the Islands. The islands down south beckon to the tourists and visitors, but have no need for mainland losers; especially of the whitey variety. They had enough hardships just keeping themselves alive.

The local color, as the tourists called it, included every kind of bottom feeder, loser, scammer, dodger, gambler, and thief imaginable. It was as if there was a sieve just south of Miami that shook and separated all the country's failures, holding back the normal folk, sending the dregs down the line. In spite of the potpourri of villains and ne'er-do-wells who settled to the bottom of the food chain, Key West was probably one of the best places in the tropics to vacation and visit. Tens of thousands of visitors poured through Key West every year, taking advantage of the huge coral reef surrounding the island for diving and fishing. The Creole atmosphere of Old Town and Duval Street was home to artists, writers, good shopping, and excellent restaurants and bars. The annual Fantasy Fest drew over a hundred thousand people down for a week in October for drinking, eating, and orgies, leaving behind a town hung over and sore. If a travel agent had to describe Key West in just a few words, they would say that it was a party version of an old Wild West town — Dodge City in flip flops.

Jack Marsh owned the Sand Bar, a watering hole on the corner of Duval and Eaton in the heart of Key West's Old Town. Jack had bought the place a little over four years ago and planned to stay there until he died, or his ex-wife found out where he was. He developed the habit of looking over his shoulder often, on the off chance that she would show up someday with either a gun or the law ... or both. The last time Jack had seen his wife, she was bent over a saddle rack in her daddy's stables playing hide the jalapeño with one of the Mexican stable boys. He watched for a couple of minutes as she squealed and squirmed in pleasure, then went back to the house, took the keys to her Mercedes and drove off. The next stop was the bank. He closed out his account where he had stashed side-money he had skimmed off his father-in-law's crooked stock scams, took all of his wife's jewelry out of the safety deposit box they shared, along with stock and bond certificates, dumped it all into a briefcase, and headed home. He called his wife's father, who was a miserable prick, and told him to shove his token job up his blue-blooded butt and that he could have his daughter back, as of that day.

"What do you mean? You can't quit. I own you. I've spent a fortune grooming you to take over the company. Get your ass back over here and tell Laura to let you in immediately when you arrive."

"No dice, Pops. This gig is over. I've had enough of you and your whole family. I married your daughter like you asked, I worked like a slave building up the business and the only thing I have ever gotten in return is a backhanded insult calling me the wise-ass punk who knocked up your daughter."

"That's a lie. I've treated you like I would my own son, Jack. I took you off the street and gave you a future," the old man screamed.

"Stop right there, Ernie. If I recall, it was me who almost went to prison because of your dumb-ass scheme to cook the books and not tell me. That little hiccup in our relationship was saved only because you put up the cash for the legal team to save my ass. I swear if I had gone to prison because of you, I would have killed you the same day I was paroled. Without me, it would have been just a matter of time before you would have been on the street, or worse, in prison. So don't give me that crap about any fatherly affection. You're also the one who came begging to me to let you use The Sand Bar to wash all that cash you cheated your clients out of. Yeah, it was a good plan using my bar, and my share was fair, so I went along with it. I was also poking your daughter at the same time, so it all looked like a win-win for me. Then she pulled that phony 'the rabbit died bullshit' and said it was mine. Hell, she was screwing every guy in Santa Barbara behind my back at the time. Then after the wedding. she announces, 'false alarm, a mix up at the clinic, Bugs Bunny didn't die after all.'"

Jack had held his tongue over the years, but the venom came tumbling out. He was on a roll now and breathing hard, "As we speak, your daughter is at your house nailing the stable boy. Last week it was the mailroom kid, the week before that it was some other guy, I don't need this ... *Ernie?*" Jack heard choking and grunts, "*Ernie?* What's wrong ... oh crap."

Jack hung up the phone and was tempted to head over to the office, but then, why should he? The old man had a bad heart, what could he do? The only reason he had stuck around was because it was easier staying than it would be moving on and starting over. Now was his chance to put the past ten years behind him and disappear.

That was almost five years ago, and he never regretted leaving one bit. Sure enough, the old man had had a heart attack and was found sprawled on his office floor, his cigar smoldering on the expensive carpet, his two-grand tailored suit soiled, and his little hairpiece askew. Sophie, his daughter, inherited a company that was so overextended that within a few months it was gone/ She was penniless. And from what a friend had told Jack, she was looking for him and her jewelry. *Good luck.*

—

Jack was counting the cash drawer, making sure the till had enough small bills to cover the needed change for the day when Arturo, his parrot, started screeching, whistling, and singing from his perch at the end of the bar. Jack had adopted Arturo when a friend died a couple of years ago from cancer. Jimmy made him swear that he would take the bird and care for it until it died or Jack died. Jack swore, and shortly after, became the proud father of the foulest mouthed, most disgusting, dirty, moody, unfriendly, hateful … bird that had ever lived in the islands. The only human Arturo liked was Coco Duvalier, Jack's right hand woman who kept the Sand Bar out of trouble and in the black.

Coco had rolled into Key West a year after Jack, turning tricks on Duval along with dozens of other hookers working the tourist trade. The local cops turned their heads for a few dollars kicked back from the girls every night. Then again, on a slow night, a patrol car would be spotted in a back alley bouncing rhythmically as one of the girls made her payment a little more personal. Coco was tall, very light skinned, had a luscious body and emerald green eyes that set her apart from her coworkers. She was one of those natural beauties that the Islands produced from the different blood lines mixed over the centuries — part African, part French, a little Spanish, and all beauty.

One night the rain was coming down in sheets, with lightning breaking across the town and thunder shaking the eaves. She asked Jack if she could stand inside the doors out of the rain and promised not to hit on any of the customers in return. She never left. Jack had always been a softy, so at closing time he asked if she had a place to stay and she said no. He told her to take the storage room and use the women's room for her private needs. The next morning, he went down to find Coco scrubbing the cold box where all the beer and perishables were kept. The bar shined from a good waxing and the floors had been mopped to a drill sergeant's satisfaction. Since then, she had been there from opening to closing time, running the day-to-day details of ordering, bill paying, buying, and banking. The only time she ever left the place was to go to her small garage apartment off Julia Street, and once a month she would take the bus up to Miami for an overnight stay.

"What do you think, Jack? Should we put the tables out front?" Coco asked, eyeing the sky.

"Yeah, let's go ahead and set 'em up. The *Princess Seas* docks in an hour. The harbor office reports there's twenty-two hundred coming ashore. Let's catch what we can," Jack said.

Jack was busy checking the icemaker when Anthony Cona and his bodyguard, Junior, came in and sat at their usual place against the far wall, close to the small bandstand.

"Hey. Mr. Cona, top of the morning to you," Jack called out, just like every morning. He could set his watch by Tony's arrival.

"So Jacky, come over here," Tony Cona said, softly motioning with his old gnarled hand.

Jack dutifully walked over, wiping his hands on a bar towel.

"You know what I want?"

"Yes sir, espresso with a whiskey on the side," Jack said, just like every morning.

"Jacky, you're good, kid, You Italian?"

"No sir, Irish."

"Hey Junior, hear that? Jacky says he's Irish. What the fuck we doing in here? He's going to fucking poison me, the fucking Mick!" The old man laughed loudly.

"Yes sir, Mr. Cona. I'll check the espresso. Jacky ain't going to get us this morning, are you Jacky?" Junior said, as they all laughed.

"No sir, not me. Every night when I go to bed, Mr. Cona, I pray I'll wake up Italian, honest," Jack said contritely.

The old man held out his hand for Jack to kiss, just like every other morning. This always seemed to mollify the old man, who immediately started mumbling and drifting off. Junior devotedly wiped drool from the senile old Mafia Don's face.

"Thanks Jack, the old man is getting worse. It won't be too much longer," Junior said, before bending to his task.

———

Jack went back to the bar to finish scooping ice into the deep stainless chests used for chilling bottles of Corona and Dos XX's so they would be tooth-freezing cold when the tourists started to pour in. Jack liked the old Don and often wondered why he was there in Key West. The only reason would be that he was banished from the crime family, or just too old to be a threat to anyone up north. The guy who owned the place before Jack said one day the Don was having his morning espresso and a couple of Jersey goomba's came in and had a whispered discussion, with the Don doing all the talking. The two mutts genuflected and kissed his hand before quickly leaving. A few minutes later, the Don went back into his stupor mode.

"Watch out for that old snake, Jack. I think his fangs are still sharp," he had said in warning.

Jack remembered in the Marines when word came down that the regiment was going to Kuwait and would be in the vanguard on the run-up against the Republican Guard. Half a dozen guys suddenly began faking mental illnesses to get out of going. The salty old Sergeant Major told them tough shit, and threatened to put them all on point leading into Kuwait City … mental illnesses ceased. Perhaps the situation was similar with the old Don.

Jack hired his kitchen help from the Florida Prison's Key West Work-Release House off of Roosevelt. So far he had been lucky, with only one case of attitude to deal with. A little short guy reported over one morning and informed Jack that he was sent against his wishes, didn't plan to work hard and, if Jack didn't like it, he could send him back, but first he was going to kick his ass.

Jack grabbed the boy's throat and squeezed, pulled him into the walk-in refrigerator off the kitchen, got up in his face, and asked, "You like pretty women?"

"Duh! What do you think? That's all I think about up in the joint, is getting me some bitches when I get out. Hell yes, I like women... no, I l-o-v-e women," he spelled out while giving his crotch an exaggerated tug.

Jack had to laugh at the answer and let him go, pushing him back onto a beer keg.

"Listen to me, Mr. Lamont. You try that tough guy crap with me, I'll cut you up and hang you over in the corner on a meat hook, you understand?" Jack said with his war face on. "What I want you to do is keep the tables clean, clear away dirty dishes, and make sure the customers are happy. While you're wiping, you can look at all the women you want, but don't touch. You touch, I'll kick *your* ass. Can you do that?"

"Why, you think I'm dumb, I can't do something that simple? Just show me where I get my white jacket. Those tables be so clean you see yourself in 'em ... and them bitches be calling out for Lamont to clean 'em some more," he boasted.

Lamont turned out to be one of the best busboys and all around dependable employees Jack had. He was quite the ladies' man. too, flirting with all the older women who came in off the ships, not to mention the big tips given to him for his attentiveness. One night business was slow, Coco had gone home with a cold, and Lamont and Jack were shooting the breeze. Jack asked him what he had done to get thrown into the joint. Lamont said that he had found a wallet stuffed with credit cards and money and went on a spending spree. By the time the cards were maxed out and the cash gone, he had spent close to fifteen thousand dollars. The D.A. told him to plead guilty and he would talk to the judge to get a walk on the prison time. So, he pled guilty, the judge threw a ten-year bounce on the kid, and he was off to the big leagues. Lamont was seventeen and homeless at the time. Lesson learned. Only the rich walk. His parole officer asked Jack if he would accept responsibility for Lamont when his release from the halfway-house came up, and he gladly accepted. He was glad for his decision to back the younger man. Sometimes people fell on hard luck and just need someone to believe in them.

—

Lamont was in back helping with the beer delivery, pulling cases of beer and tap kegs, when Pointman walked in. Pointman didn't actually walk like most people. He did more like a jitter step, kind of like his body was constantly shaking and looked like one of those windup toys that vibrate across the floor without actually moving any appendages. He vibrated over to the bar.

"H ... Hey J ... Jack, 'z ... z'up man," he stuttered, pulling out a pack of smokes and shaking one out.

Jack held a match to the cigarette and after a couple of tries; Point got his jittering rhythm down, lit up, and inhaled deeply. Jack blew out the match and shoved the packet across the bar.

"Hey Point, how they hanging this morning?" Jack asked as he placed an ashtray on the bar.

Pointman took a deep drag and blew out forcefully, "I … I'm scared … Jack, I th …think I stepped into some sh … shit last night."

"Hey, you smell ok," Jack said smiling, giving him the once over.

Point had lived on the streets and alleys of Key West for years/ Some say he showed up sometime after the Tet offensive in Vietnam back in the sixties, but no one knew for sure. It was known that he was an outpatient at the V.A. in the Navy annex and should be living there. But the rooms and the money were going to the younger men from Iraq and Afghanistan, so he lived on the streets. Jack gave him a few bucks every now and then and let him sleep in the storeroom on stormy nights. Somewhere between Pointman's Vietnam tour and coming home, he lost his mind and you never knew if you were talking to the stealthy Pointman on jungle patrol or the spaced out mindless caricature he is today.

"Ja … Jack, I … saw a man ge … get killed la … last night, sw … swear to Go … God!"

"Killed! Where?"

"Ov … over by the bi … big warehouse on Whii … Whii … off Mustin. Yo … you know the one b … by the Coast G … Guard Sta … sta … Base."

"Sure, the big one that used to be part of the Navy Base, yeah I know which one."

"I was set-in fo … for the night, boo … booby traps out, ni … night fi … fire on ca … call behind a du … dumpster. I was ready man, Charlie hit the wire, and I was ready. Know what I mean?"

"Yeah, I'm with you."

"A … about 02:00, one of them pig cans pulled in and parks ten meters to my front."

"Pig can?" Jack asked.

"Yeah, one of them fed plain-wrap cars the pigs drive around trying to fool people cause there ain't no signs on 'em," Point said matter-of-factly. "They pull up and cut the m … motor, and I hear talking. Somebody smacked someone and cussed him out real loud. One of them guys called the other a fart-knocker and I just about cracked up. I ain't heard that since I was a kid in Waco. The other guy was crying and saying he wasn't trying to double cross anyone. It was all a misunderstanding, and that he had the money in a safe place."

As Jack listened, it occurred to him that Point had lost his jittery speech and was coherent. Jack could tell Point was afraid by the way he would look over his shoulder to see if anyone was watching or coming for him. Jack ran a draft beer for him and Point sucked it down in two gulps, wiped his mouth, and continued, "Then they really started screaming back and forth. I could hear slaps and fists hitting flesh. Somebody was getting beat good. Then a shot went off and scared the shit out of me and I lost it," he said, eyes huge in his head. "I could see a platoon of gooks coming through the wire and I started throwing grenades and hollering 'Gooks in the wire! Gooks in the wire!' I know it was just my imagination, but it seemed so real. I didn't have no grenades, either. I had an old bucket filled with limes I picked over off Elizabeth Street, and was throwing those at the pigs. I guess I must have scared them, because they dumped a body out of that car and hauled ass." He stopped to wipe his mouth and pointed to his empty glass for a refill.

"I got the price for it, Jack/ Run me one," he said.

Jack tapped off the glass, set it in front of Point, and was surprised when he pulled out a huge roll of money. Point peeled off a hundred and said, "That's the smallest I got, sorry."

"Pointman, where the hell did you get that money, man? There must be five or six thousand bucks in that roll," Jack said. Jack had never seen Point with any money, except loose change that he panhandled off tourists.

"I got it off the dead man, Jack. After them shooters left, I checked on the body to see if the guy was alive. Sure enough, he was dead, so I checked for ID and came up with this money, ain't it beautiful?" he beamed. "Hey, and check these out," he said, pointing to a pair of expensive hand-tooled cowboy boots. "Ain't they beauties? And fit good too."

Pointman swiveled his head around to see if anyone was looking, "I got this too," he said, laying a .38 automatic on the bar along with a key on an ID chain.

Jack scooped up the pistol and put it under the bar before someone saw it and got nosey.

"Point, what happened next? Did you call the law?"

"The Law! Jack are you fucking nuts? The law ain't going to believe anything I say. Hell naw, man. I took the dead guy's stuff and dee dee'ed out of there, dude," he said in a rush. "I been on the run all night waiting to come see you for help. I spent the night on the roof over at Sears Town. My stuff is still up there, and I ain't going back unless you say to. Jack, those pigs saw me, they know who I am. I'm scared," he said, looking over his shoulder for gunmen to come barging in.

"Take it easy, Point, no one is going to bother you here," Jack said and drew another beer for him.

Just as he took a long pull on his glass, Arturo cut loose with a loud, "*Show me your stuff, Show me your stuff,*" from the other end of the bar, causing Point to spew beer in fright all over Jack and the bar.

"Jeezus, that frigging bird scairt the pee out of me!" Point said. "Jack, that frigging parrot hates me. Every time I come in, it smarts off to me. I never sh … sh … should have sh … shown hi … him nuthen' the first time it asked."

Coco rushed over to wipe the bar and laughed at Point's comment about the time Arturo had yelled out, *"Show me your stuff,"* and a drugged-out Point dropped his drawers and hung it out for all the bar customers to see. Arturo went into an immediate braying of *"Heehaw, Heehaw, Heehaw!"* Since then, Point hated Arturo, and vice versa.

Jack threw Arturo a maraschino cherry out of the well to shut him up. The bird caught it with one foot, and yelled back, "Out!" *Crazy damn bird.* Jack was disgusted that he didn't know that parrots lived to be in their late thirties to early forties when he had agreed to adopt him. Having the damn bird was like living with a delinquent teenager all your life — he was always a smartass with the last word.

"What should I do, Jack?" Point asked.

"Well, for now, go upstairs and get cleaned up. Take a snooze, and later we'll take a cab over to get your gear off the Sears' roof, and then we'll see."

Jack lived upstairs in a small four-room place he had tricked out to look like a scene from a tropical catalog. Jack had always loved Key West and the island architecture, which was a mix of all the different countries that ruled the islands at one time or another over the centuries, leaving behind their influence in style and colors, not to mention bloodlines. Linguists have studied the island's Creole language for years and found word traces of almost every European nation and African tribe there is. If you haven't grown up speaking the island language, you will never fully understand what is being said. dialects within dialects, within slang, within tones …

Jack led Point upstairs after another beer to calm his nerves, laid out some old jeans and a shirt for him to put on after a hot shower, and headed back down to the bar. "Stay out of the fridge, and don't touch the grouper that's marinating on the counter. That's my dinner," Jack warned on his way down the stairs.

"Hey Jack, I'm rich now. if I wanted grouper, I'd get me some, I don't need you to feed me. Hell, I might just go over to the Raw Bar and get a couple dozen oysters later on."

"No way, we're putting that roll of cash in the locker downstairs for safe keeping. You flash that wad around town, and you'll be a crispy critter in no time. I'll hang on to it and you can take whatever you need whenever you want. Just don't go flashing it or talking about it."

"You're right, Jack. You're the only one I can trust, except for Black Alice. She's always good to me when I need to talk to somebody besides those shrinks out at the V.A. Hell

Jack, those boys out there don't even speak English. One of those docs is Vietnamese, for Christ's sake. How is he going to straighten me out, I ask you? The damn Congs are the ones that made me this way," Point said, mystified at the system that he was caught up in.

Jack warned Point to stay put and bounced down the outside stairs, picking up the beat of *Margaretville* being belted out by the Sand Bar's very own Johnny Boofey. That's his name, or at least the stage name that he went by. Johnny sounded more like Jimmy Buffett than Jimmy Buffett did, and he packed the customers in with his act. Johnny could damn near imitate any country or rock singer who ever recorded. The real Jimmy Buffett's place was a couple blocks farther down, and Jack was sure that one day Jimmy Buffett would come down with his guys armed with baseball bats and beat the crap out of everyone in the place. Johnny worked for minimum wage, plus tips and sales of his discs, plus all the drinks the customers bought him. By closing time every night, Johnny was hoarse from singing and falling-down drunk. His girlfriend, Sonja, would scrape him up, pour him into a cab, and they'd drive off in a cloud of coral dust.

Jack paused for a moment out in the alley, caught by the sight of little dervish cyclones of coral dust blowing trash into the air. The sky was darkening with purplish bruise-colored clouds scuttling in from the southeast, pushed by the trade winds blowing up from Puerto Rico. The smell of salt and rain lay heavy over the city, thunder rolled way off, sounding like cannon broadsides from a long gone era in a duel to the death. He was worried about his partner Tommy Hicks. This would not be a good night to be caught out on the blue.

Chapter 2

Tommy Hicks watched the deep cobalt blue rollers, pushed by the storm, coming up from the southeast. *The Island Girl*, an old forty-eight-foot dive boat converted for salvage and commercial diving, rode the swells gracefully, rising and falling almost in tune to the slow-motion samba rhythm blaring out of the boat's radio tuned to Radio Havana. Tommy sat at anchor off Screaming Woman Key, twenty miles south of Key West, with fishing line spooled out, waiting for Miguel Santos to arrive for their weekly rendezvous. The *Girl's* radar had a vessel coming up from the south that wasn't squawking any identification, which isn't too unusual for watercraft coming out of Cuba, especially with a storm moving in. Santos would be there, Tommy knew for sure. He had never missed a meet-up yet, and there was too much money in it for the Cuban not to show. Every Wednesday for three years, the two men met out in the Florida Straight, passing black market goods over to the Cubans in exchange for cash.

It had started simply enough, with Miguel Santos bringing his Cuban Navy patrol boat up alongside *The Girl*, tying off, and making himself at home aboard her. Tommy was on the bottom, in ninety feet of water, picking over the bones of an old cargo vessel that had sunk a few years before and was so engrossed in his find that he didn't even know another boat had joined him. When Tommy came up, he found Miguel sitting in his captain's chair, kicked back, and smoking a cigar. After a few minutes of macho B.S. about boarding without permission outside territorial waters and CIA spy accusations, the two backed down from name calling and threats. One thing led to another and soon the two men were talking about things men always talk about, women, gambling, baseball, and more women. The friendship was sealed when Carlos told Tommy he had been in the Cuban Naval Brigade — Marine Brigade — and had fought in Angola in the late seventies as a sergeant. Tommy told of his stint as a corporal in the Marines in Kuwait and the bond was made, *Brothers in Arms*. Later, as the two relaxed on the aft deck sharing a bucket of crab claws along with cold beer, they hatched the plan to start a black market operation where the two could get rich, as long as they didn't get greedy or careless. It started out with auto parts — spark plugs, distributors, generators, windshield wipers — basic stuff, all in huge demand throughout the island. They soon expanded into electronics and appliances. Miguel's position of Squadron Capitán for the Santa Cruz Del Norte Coastal Patrol allowed him to move freely and unquestioned, and Tommy's salvage and dive business gave him free access to just about anywhere he wanted to go without any hassle from the Coast Guard or suspicious DEA agents. It was a win-win setup.

The NOAA weather report on channel 16 had issued a small craft warning hours ago and said that the tropical depression was sinking fast and could shoot up to a Cat 1 hurricane by midnight. Tommy wasn't concerned yet. he could pull the hook and be back at the dock faster than the storm could move, but still, he didn't like taking any chances out there. It was for this very reason that he had been able to make a living off salvage work out in the Strait. Storms could come up very fast, catch the unprepared skipper by surprise, and take him to the bottom. Actually, big storms were good for Tommy's business, especially leisure craft that went down with all hands ... usually families or partiers out having fun, and not knowing the danger signs.

"*Island Girl, Island Girl,* this is Cuban Patrol niner nine. Come in please."

"Yo, niner-nine, this is *the Girl.*"

"*Girl,* my E.T.A. is ten minutes. Stand by with papers, Señor."

That was the standard line to tell Tommy that all was ok and that Miguel was on his way. It also gave Tommy cover with the Coast Guard if ever questioned why he was tied-up alongside a Cuban Navy vessel.

The two men were standing out of the light rain, under the canvas Biminis that stretched over half the aft deck of *The Girl.* Miguel had his crew tie up alongside *The Girl,* and within minutes of arriving, started shifting the contraband aboard and below decks of his vessel. Tommy never asked about the loyalty of Miguel's crew and really didn't have any need to know. They were Miguel's problem, but they all seemed to respect him and responded quickly to his commands. Today's pickup was going to be Tommy's most profitable shipment to date. It consisted of handheld GPS units, satellite cell phones, and sixty-minute phone cards. He would clear 15K today, cash.

"Drugs! You're nuts, Miguel! There is no frigging way we should start dealing in drugs. That'll have the DEA on our ass in a New York minute," Tommy said.

"Thomas, don't you see? This is a big opportunity for us. We deal in this *little* stuff and we stay *little*. We go to drugs we will soon be millionaires, compadre," Miguel said, eyes twinkling with a larcenous grin on his face. "I have a customer who will supply all the drugs we can deliver for him. I give you the drugs out here on the blue and you deliver them to my friend's Miami people dockside in Key West, simple, yes? They give you the money and you bring it out here with you the next day."

"Simple, no. You're asking for trouble, Miguel. Castro and his boys will string you up by your cajones when they catch you."

"Thomas, my friend, I am not a hero. I am a coward. Even though you and I make good money doing our little business, most of mine goes to the big boys in Havana to look the other way. No, my friend, these drugs are not for Cuba and the revolution," Miguel laughed. "They are for a friend of a friend in Cancun, a businessman with great wealth who deals in drugs. Here, I have schedule of deliveries and drop offs," he said, pulling out a folded piece of notebook paper.

Tommy's hand shook as he read the handwritten schedule.

"Holy shit, Miguel!" Tommy swore. "The first delivery is tomorrow night. No fucking way can we do this. Even if I knew anything about the drug trade, the feds would be all over us. We need to walk away from this and leave drug-running to the big guys. Remember, we agreed we would never become greedy, and this kind of greed will get us dead, partner."

"Thomas, I am sorry to say, but we don't have a choice. If it were me, I would agree with you that we are doing very well with our little business. My life is good, my wife gets fatter every day, my children do not go without, my mother and father are comfortable compared to our fellow Cubans. No it is not my wish. I have been told to make this thing happen, or I will be turned over to the authorities for selling contraband goods and will be sent before a firing squad." He paused, "And you Thomas, will be reported to your authorities to be dealt with," Miguel said apologetically. "We must deliver on this soon, my friend, or the hammer will fall on both of us."

"Who's behind this? Just tell them we can't do it, for Christ's sake. I swear Miguel, I don't want any part of this and I know I speak for Jack as well. He would never go along with this. Besides, if we did run drugs for this friend of a friend, once we do, they will own us forever and we just become mules for their wants. We'll be no better off than a couple of dogs that obey when their master whistles."

"Thomas, there is more. This thing is already in motion. You and I are actually very small potatoes in this. The reason I was late today is because my friend called on me and gave me instructions. He told me that I must get you to agree with being part of this, and, if you did not agree, I was to kill you …"

"*Miguel!* What the fuck are you saying? If I say no … you're going to kill me?"

"No, no, Thomas, I am not going to kill you … *he* said to kill you. I didn't say *I* would. You are my friend and business partner. How can I kill you? We are small- time businessmen, not killers. The schedule I just gave to you, I made up. There is no schedule. I needed to see if you would go for it before I told you the truth."

"Miguel, I just can't do it, I'm no criminal. Sure, we make a few bucks on this penny-ante crap, but hell, it's like humanitarian work, supplying all those poor Cubans with stuff. But drugs, that's big league … count me out, I mean it."

"Thomas, if I count you out, then I am killing my own family and me. These bastards don't take no for an answer. If you say yes, and then don't come through, they will kill my fat wife, my little girls, and me. I swear, we are fucked."

"Did your friend tell you that? Did he say he would kill you and your family if I didn't go along with it?" Tommy asked, anguish crushing his face.

"*Si, Hermano, mi familia está muerta* — my family is dead if you don't go along. I am sorry, Thomas. I am sorry that I have gotten you into this."

Both men sat quietly thinking of the danger they had found themselves in, and couldn't get out of.

"Even if I say yes, I don't know who these Miami people are. I won't know if I'm dealing with the druggies or the DEA."

"That is it, my friend," Miguel said exhaling loudly, hands on knees, "We do not have to do anything but deliver the cargo. Someone will approach you in Key West and arrange to load up your boat with money. Then you meet me out here and I take the money and you take the drugs. The money goes with me into Santa Cruz and it is offloaded and disappears, later arriving in Isla Mujeres, off Cancun. That is all I know."

"Oh man, this is going to be so fucking dangerous. There is no way we can keep this a secret for long. The Coast Guard and DEA let me fly under the radar because I am harmless, but drugs … oh dude, they are going to light me up. *And,* if the FBI gets involved, then we are really fucked. Those guys shoot first and talk later."

"It is indeed a big risk to us, Thomas. I think we need to go along for now and see what we can do to escape from these putas."

"What are they going to pay us?"

"Pay? We get to live, that's our pay."

Chapter 3

A torrent of rain slapped the sidewalk and street as the storm front tore through Key West. Bloated storm clouds roiled low overhead as megaton watts of lightning shot down, blinding the eye. Nano-seconds later, explosions of thunder blasted shock waves through brick and flesh alike. Duval Street was empty except for a few drunks frolicking in the downpour. The streets and gutters were awash with runoff that was quickly overloading the sewer system, and the street lights had come on, fooled by the faux darkness of the evening. In spite of the explosive wrath of the storm, you could almost feel the city sigh in relief from the tropical heat that had baked it for far too long, drinking up the precious moisture like a wino sucking up his first fifth of the day.

Jack was sitting at the end of the bar closest to the front, watching the storm create a wet kaleidoscope of color from the reflections of all the neon lights up and down Duval. Johnny Boofey's singing was in serious competition with the rain beating down on the sidewalk's tin-roof overhang and finally gave up, amped his guitar to afterburner level, and busted into his Carlos Santana imitation. The place was packed with vacation visitors staying at the local hotels and B&B's, determined to drink the bar dry and consume iced shrimp and greasy cheeseburger baskets until Rome burned down. Most of the ship's passengers had pulled up anchor and deserted the island a couple of hours earlier, sailing off into the gathering storm, while the stranded ones just partied on while a designated cruiser fretted over arranging flights to hook up with the ship at its next port of call. *Oh, the sweet life a credit card provides!*

Jack was worried about Tommy being out on the water in this storm and couldn't figure out why he hadn't docked and checked in yet. Tommy knew these local waters like the back of his hand and never took chances, especially when it came to *The Girl*. He loved that boat more than he loved anything. If he could figure out a way to knock her up, he would. *Nobody* messed with *The Girl*! She was his home, his job, his hobby, and his lover.

Jack thought he was probably just overreacting, but still, this was a big storm. Even if he anchored up somewhere, it was one hell of a blow. Tommy and Jack were old Marine buddies from the Kuwait invasion back in the day, when old Storm'n Norman out-fought and out-flanked Hussein's elite Republican Guard and sent them down the Highway of Death by the thousands to meet Allah. They had been in the same fire team with Delta Company and Seventh Marines when the unit entered Kuwait City. The Marines came under heavy fire immediately, but kept the pressure on, making good headway, fighting street by street, when suddenly Jack and Tommy came under withering automatic gunfire and ducked into a building for cover. The building turned out to be a bank, and the next thing they knew, they were in the bank's basement shooting locks off safety deposit boxes and stuffing cash and jewels in their rucks. Meanwhile, the rest of their platoon had advanced a few more blocks when it was discovered that they were missing. The Platoon Sergeant spotted them running towards him, lugging coin sacks filled with money and jewels, happy as drunken sailors. The two Corporals tried to explain they were going to share with all the other guys in the platoon. But after the Marines had taken the city, they each were busted to the rank of Private, and did thirty days in the brig aboard ship. Chickenshit Lieutenant … *yeah, the Marines have them too.*

Once the unit returned to the U.S., the incident was forgotten and the two received Honorable Discharges with the brig time having been deleted from their record books, but only because of the Battalion's Sergeant Major going to the wall for them. In fact, the old salty Sergeant Major told them that they had screwed up and should have dug a hole somewhere and gone back later to get the booty. After they had returned and mustered out, Tommy headed for Florida to party and drink the dust and sand out of his craw. When he heard that Key West was the place to be for spring break and wild chicks, he was on his way. When he sobered up, he worked jobs bussing tables and bartending until his Sheriff's Department application was approved, and then headed off to the Sheriff's Academy to become one of Monroe County's finest. A year later, Tommy was hit by a drunk driver while making a routine traffic stop out on Highway One and was forced to give up his job. Jack and Tommy were like brothers, watched out for each other through good and bad times, and were always looking for ways to make a quick buck. When Jack walked away from Santa Barbara, leaving his wife bent over a saddle bench, his father-in-law lying on the floor dying and a briefcase full of cash and jewels, he knew exactly where he was going. Jack stashed some of the cash, sold the jewels and put a chunk down on the bar — which he quickly christened The Sand Bar — then went partners with Tommy, putting up the down payment on the *Island Girl*, on which Tommy had been working as a deckhand running scuba divers out to the Dry Tortugas.

"Show me your junk, Show me your junk!" Arturo screamed loudly, as a couple of middle-aged women drunkenly raised their tank-tops flashing their boobs to the yelling and clapping crowd.

"Put 'em away, Put 'em away!" Arturo screamed, and quickly ducked his head under his wing to fend off french-fries and pieces of ice thrown at him from the boozy crowd. That bird was going to get himself killed one of these nights, and then the bar would be stuck with a ton of Arturo T-shirts and cups with his ugly mug on them with his famous "Show

Me Your Junk" shtick silkscreened on them. The souvenir business was like printing money, what with everyone looking for a cheap reminder of what a great time they had in Key West. Almost like a symbol of survival that their friends back home could look on in envy. The little souvenir shop did as much as the bar did on a good day, selling everything from Sand Bar hats to key chains to plush stuffed Arturo parrots from China at outrageous prices.

—

It was about 11:00 p.m. and the storm was still ripping through town when Bill Short stuck his head through the kitchen door motioning for Jack to come over. Jack thought maybe Bill had stopped by to grab a cheeseburger off the cuff and just wanted to say hi.

"Hey, Billy what's up, man? Good night for bad guys, huh?" Jack said as he stepped into the kitchen letting the swinging doors close behind him.

"Jack, I have a situation on my hands and need to talk to you," Billy said and stepped over by the back door, motioning Jack to follow.

"Sure, what can I do for Monroe County's finest?" Billy and Tommy had been close in the Sheriff's Department before Tommy's accident.

"Wendell Chalmers was found shot to death about an hour ago. His body was discovered behind one of the mausoleums in the cemetery."

"Ok, but what does this have to do with me?" Jack asked trying to put a face to someone named Wendell Chalmers and coming up blank.

"Wendell Chalmers is Pointman, Jack. The old Vietnam Vet who hangs around town. His body was beat up pretty bad, stabbed several times, then had one planted in the forehead. Your bicycle was found a few graves over, plus a book of matches with the Sand Bar logo imprint on them was found close to the body. Lieutenant Mathers sent me over to bring you in for questioning —"

"Hold on, Billy, Pointman is upstairs in my place. I let him go up there to clean up earlier this afternoon and to sit out the storm."

"Jack," Lamont called out, "I got busy and forgot to tell you. Pointman cut out about three hours ago and borrowed your bike. Said he had to go get his gear from Sears Town. He asked me to tell you that he would be back later and that he would be watching out for the Cong."

Jack felt a cold chill run up his back, and then, just as fast, the disbelief that Pointman was dead hit him. *Hell, we were just talking only a few hours ago. I just gave him fresh clothes and a place to hide ... oh crap! It's the money he took off the dead man, or maybe he was hit because the shooters thought he would turn them in for killing the guy with the boots. But why, then, torture him before killing him? Did he know something else that he didn't tell me?* Jack quickly decided to keep all this secret for now, until he learned a little more about what was going on.

"Let me grab a rain jacket and we can get going," Jack said, going out the back and up the stairs, trying to avoid the rain pelting him.

At the top of the landing to the small porch-patio, Jack skidded to a stop. The front door was wide open. Goose bumps chilled him as they ran up and down his back and neck. He moved slowly over to the door and peeked inside. It was dark except for the light coming from the bedroom windows up front. Jack could feel that there was someone waiting for him behind the door. He took a quick breath and jumped inside, doing his best karate *Yaeee ya,* hitting the light switch at the same time. Two huge alley cats screamed in fright and jumped down from the kitchen counter where they had been feasting on the grouper a la marinade, and dashed out, escaping into the rain.

"Dirty bastards," Jack yelled after them. "That was my dinner, you pussies!" Jack said, shutting the door. He went to the bathroom and was wiping his face and hair when he noticed wet shoe tracks on the hall floor leading into the bedroom. He flipped off the bathroom light and stood listening for any sound. It was impossible to hear anything with the rain beating down on the tin roof, so he tiptoed into the room and flipped on the lights. The wet splotches stopped a couple of feet inside the room and then apparently, whoever it was backed out. This was creeping him out even after checking under the bed and in the closet. Jack's Glock 9mm was in the bedside table right where it had been for the last four years, except for target practice with the guys every now and then. Jack left the lamp on and went back to the kitchen, tossed what was left of the grouper into a trash sack, and took it down with him to toss.

"Let's go," Jack said as he jumped into Billy's Sheriff's unit.

The wipers were beating like a high school drum line against the slanting rain and it was still almost impossible to see more than a few feet ahead of the unit. Billy had his emergency bar lights flicking for safety and steered down the middle of Eaton Street. Sane people were inside out of the rain, but the occasional cluster of visitors weren't losing a minute of their holiday time and rode their rented motor scooters like water bugs through the dark flooded streets, splashing spray on each other, daring Mother Nature to screw with their vacation.

"Billy, how come the Sheriff is handling this? Shouldn't the Key West cops be in charge since it's on their turf?"

"Well, I'm not sure how it was worked out. But because there is a strong chance that this could be gang related, the city asked for the Sheriff to take the lead."

"Gang related? I didn't know that we had any big gang problems here. The police do a good job of keeping the locals under control and have a good community outreach program. Hell, I give them money every year for their athletic programs and donate money for team uniforms. I get a nice plaque in return showing their appreciation."

"It's not the locals the boss is worried about. The bullet to the forehead, execution style, is usually associated with the big drug gangs from up on the mainland. The Sheriff and the Chief don't want those guys getting a foothold down here if they can stop it early, so we work as a team. That way it also keeps the Feebs and the DEA clowns from muscling in and screwing things up. We want to keep control locally, unless we really can't solve something ourselves. Besides, this is the second murder in two days with the same M.O."

The first stop was at the Key West Medical Center on Stock Island where Billy wanted Jack to identify Pointman's remains for the record. It took less than five minutes to identify the body and sign the papers acknowledging that the body shown to him was indeed one Wendell "Pointman" Chalmers. It wasn't easy looking at Point. Whoever had done this to him was going for effect and pain. Unless they were psychotic and got off on inflicting pain, this was an interrogation torture meant to get information. Why else the shallow knife cuts and stab wounds? It suddenly occurred to Jack that they may have beaten him to find out who he had told about the murder, and, once he told them, they popped him in the forehead.

"What did you tell them, Point? Are they heading my way?" Jack said in a whisper as he stood looking down at a sleeping Pointman.

"Pardon, Jack? What did you say?"

"Nothing. Billy, just a little prayer," Jack said. "What happens to him now?"

"As soon as the Sheriff is satisfied with the autopsy report, he'll be released to whoever comes to claim him."

"And if no one comes?"

"He goes to research at one of the state med schools, I guess."

"I don't want that to happen. If no one comes, I'll pay any funeral and burial costs. Maybe we can put him in one of the National Cemeteries around the country. I think he would like that, being with his buddies."

"I'll let the Sheriff know, Jack. I always said you were an old softy."

"Let's get out of here, if we're finished," Jack said, then stopped. "Where are Point's belongings?"

"Belongings? He didn't have anything on but a pair of baggy skivvy drawers with your name stenciled in them. He was splayed out across one of those above ground graves looking for all the world like Christ brought down from the cross. It was spooky, Jack."

—

Jack got back to his place around three in the morning, exhausted from the hours of sitting and repeating everything he ever knew about Pointman, with focus on today's … yesterday's events. Lieutenant Mathers was up-front with Jack and said that he was not a suspect, but had him repeating his story in case anything new or different popped out that might give them a lead on who the shooter had been. Jack cleverly left off the part about the money and what Point had told him about the killing the night before. He also didn't share his thoughts about why Point was stripped down and left with nothing on but a pair of underwear. Could have been just an interrogation tactic to scare Point, but now he was leaning towards the killers looking for something they thought Point had. Jack was sure it was the *Pigs* that killed Point, whoever the *Pigs* were.

Jack let himself into the kitchen, flipped the lights on, and headed up front to the bar. A few neon beer signs around the large room reflected off the mirrors across the back of the bar giving a soft cozy feeling … like home. The place was spotless, with all the chairs up off the floor, turned upside down on the tables. The mahogany bar and stainless-steel sinks were shiny and clean; the glassware hung from the overhead racks ready for the next day's drinkers. Jack went back in the kitchen and fired up a burner on the stove, cracked a couple of eggs into a small skillet, sprinkled some pizza cheese and a handful of jalapeño slices into the eggs, and stirred like crazy. He grabbed a hamburger bun from the breadbox, swirled the omelet around a couple of times and flipped it onto the bread. It wasn't grouper a la marinade, but it hit the spot. Jack poured himself a big glass of cold milk from the fridge and sat at one of the prep tables to eat, thinking through the night's events. Suddenly it hit him — the key! He remembered the key. Pointman had the roll of money in his pocket ... and a key! The key! How could he have forgotten it? He rushed over to the large cold reefer where they kept the cases of beer and perishables, moved a few kegs out of the way, and entered the combo to the safe. There it was. The key lay next to the stash of money, right where he had put it. He grabbed up the key and the money, and went back out to the kitchen.

The little fob on the keychain was inscribed *KEY WEST STORAGE,* and on the flip side, Unit B260. Jack was sure he knew where the place was, but pulled the phonebook out from under the bar just to make sure. Key West was such a transient place that these storage unit places were all over town. The one he was looking for was located off Highway 1, just before you pulled into town. He remembered it being next to a huge boatyard where a guy had killed the yard owner last year for repossessing his boat because he was three months behind on his payments. A shootout and hostage situation developed between the guy and the Sheriff's boys that ended with the guy taking fourteen rounds to the torso and the hostage nineteen rounds … sounded like a fair swap to Jack, three lives for a twenty-one foot SeaPro.

Jack splashed water on his face, grabbed the hand towel over the bathroom sink, and caught a glimpse of himself in the mirror. He looked tired and noticed the crow's feet cutting deeper around the corner of his eyes, a few more gray hairs mixed in with the black around the temples. He had enlisted in the Marines after college, weighing one-eighty, came out at two-ten, and now hit the scales at two-fifteen. Jack was a handsome man with a square jaw and chin and green Irish eyes. His teeth were still white and straight, in spite of having had a busted jaw, and he had a nasty scar that ran from mid-forehead down through his left eyebrow from a sailor in San Diego who kicked him when he was down. His ex-wife said that the scar gave him a tough, mean look when he squinted, but was cute when he smiled. Overall, not bad for a guy about to hit the big four-0 in a couple of months. He had just squirted some Visine in his eyes when his cell rang. He grabbed it off the dresser in the bedroom and flipped it open.

"Yeah?"

"It's me, I'm back in port," Tommy said, sounding tired.

"Yeah, I was getting worried. Thought maybe that Cuban cowboy had shot you or something," Jack said, trying not to sound too relieved.

"No, the storm almost got me, but me and *The Girl* kicked its ass."

"Good, tell me all about it in the morning. I think we have trouble coming our way. I'll tell you about it when I see you."

"You don't know the half of it, Jack."

Chapter 4

Jack was usually up and downstairs by seven every morning, but today it took a few more minutes before rolling out. He had finally drifted off around four into a dream-filled trance which left him more tired than before. Lamont was making a racket downstairs as he opened the big sliding front and side doors, then set out the sidewalk tables and chairs. Cookie, the fry cook and chef, was rattling pots and pans around and singing a gospel tune in his deep Creole baritone as he prepared for another busy day of cheeseburgers, fries, and a killer conch chowder made from his momma's recipe. He went through a good five gallons of the stuff on a normal day, and double that when the ships were in.

By the time Jack rolled into the office — the stool at the end of the bar — it was almost 8 o'clock. Coco was busy doing paperwork and only gave him a brief, "'Morning," and went back to her papers.

"I had to let Mary go last night," Coco said conversationally, as she ran numbers on her calculator.

"Oh?"

"Yeah, she was shorting the cash drawer. I've been watching her for a while, and if I hadn't have done it myself before, I never would have spotted her," she said, still tapping out numbers.

"Yeah?"

"Uh, huh, sure enough. About every third time she went into the cash register, she held back a couple of dollars. That doesn't sound like a lot, but as much cash as we have flowing through here, it adds up fast. Unless you're right on top of it, you aren't going to see it."

"She give you any trouble?"

"Trouble! Me? Jack, please. You know better than that. Don't worry, I have a replacement coming in this morning. She worked over at the Bird House, but quit when the boss kept hitting on her. She's going to cost us a few more dollars, but she's worth it. Big, beautiful, and blond. Dressed in our summer outfits, she's going to stop traffic out on Duval, guaranteed."

Every guy in the world knows that a little T&A sells, so when Jack took over the Sand Bar, he had all the girls wear tropical-themed halter tops and little sarongs to pull the men in … and it was an instant hit. The girls made big tips and the bar business exploded. Jack and the males wore logo Sand Bar sports polos and khaki shorts or pants. Jack chalked it up to the Marine in him. He just liked a uniform, especially a nice fitting halter top.

"Hey, if she can bring in more drinkers, she'll be worth the extra bucks."

"I don't think it's going to be drinks that bring the guys in. She goes by Barbie for a reason," Coco said with a chuckle. "A name like Karen Wilson just isn't the same kind of draw."

Jack told Coco about the events of last night and about Point, and to watch for strangers or anything out of the ordinary around the place.

"I have to run over to see Tommy and will be back in a couple of hours, so you have the helm," Jack said.

"Yeah, right. As if the place would shut down with you gone!" she said and rolled her eyes.

"That's my girl!"

"Hey, wait a minute. What do you want me to do with this gun?" She said, and held up the pistol that Point had taken off the dead man and left at the bar yesterday.

"Stick it in the receipt drawer for now until I get back," Jack told her.

The sun was burning off all the pools of rainwater left behind by the storm, making it blistery hot and humid. Jack kept to the shadows cast by the shop awnings as he hurried the two blocks to the taxi stand next to Fast Buck Freddie's Mercantile. A lone cab sat with its motor running, and frosted windows from the air conditioner blowing. Jack jumped in and gasped at the cold air.

"Hey, Jacky, long time no see," the driver said as he pulled away.

Jack couldn't place the guy's name but knew he had been around for a long time, driving a cab.

"Yeah, busy, busy, pal. How about you? Doing ok?"

"Sure, you know the score. Come see, come saw, good days, bad days, evens out," the guy lamented.

"Boy, don't I know it," Jack said, commiserating with the guy, but not having a fucking clue what they were talking about.

"Hey, did you hear about the big killing over at the cemetery last night?" the cabbie asked, not waiting for an answer. "The cops said it was horrible, some kind of sick voodoo ritual thing, hands and feet cut off, dick zippered and stuck in his mouth. The Sheriff's calling in special agents from Tallahassee, career guys that handle these kinds of atrocities. Can you believe it? In fucking America!"

"Drop me over at the Shrimp Bar, ok?"

"Sure, have you there in a jiffy. Then, if that ain't the cat's shit, word's out that there's ten million bucks stashed somewhere in town. Some limp dick heisted the cartel's weekly wash, and the mucky mucks sent down a squad of hitters to find it, even if they have to sink the island in blood. Ain't that some shit?"

Jacks antennas shot up through his skull, sending little pinballs of acid bouncing around his gut.

"No shit! Who told you all that?'

"You know I can't reveal my sources. If I told ya, I might get my throat cut. But I will tell you this, a friend of a friend who's connected with those kinds of people said so, and if he says so, then you can take it to the bank. Hey, here we are already."

"How much?" Jack asked as he pulled out his wallet.

"Give me a couple of bucks, Jacky. You're always a good customer and a good conversationalist. I always enjoy having you in the cab."

Jack gave him five and waved him off when he objected.

Seagulls were swooping down into the still harbor waters, feasting on little fish that hadn't survived last night's storm, while pelicans paddled among the larger floaters, filling their huge pouches with the tastier morsels that hadn't made the cut. It was beyond hot, and the smell of decomposing fish and sea life made it hard to breathe. The stink-saturated humidity lay heavy over the town and wouldn't burn off until midday when the coral-crushing tropical sun was at its zenith.

Jack had to force himself to breathe as he walked across the crushed oyster-shell parking lot in front of the Island Dive Shop. It was more like a shack than a shop, made to look like an old Hawaiian hula shack, with a palm frond roof and wooden porch with dive tanks and gear hanging from the storefront walls. Jack had put up the down payment when the original owner wanted to retire and offered the place to Tommy. Jack agreed to co-sign for his friend on the bank note, which included *The Island Girl*, but Tommy ran the business. Tommy took divers from the mainland out for day and night dives, but considered his primary business to be salvage and wreck reclamation. His weekly contraband trips really made it where he didn't have to do anything else if he didn't want to, but he loved the water so much you couldn't keep him off it. The bank loan was paid off early from the black market profits, and Jack pulled twenty-percent off the take as a partner in the biz, occasionally going with Tommy on the meet-ups with the Cuban, Santos.

"Yo, Tommy, where are you?" Jack yelled out.

"On the boat, come on around," he yelled back.

Tommy was swabbing the deck back and forth in big swaths as Mimi, his girlfriend, hosed the transom and dive platform off. Jack stood watching the pair and thought how perfect these two people were for each other, if they could just get their act together and agree that they were in love. Both sun-bleached blondes, deep tans burned into their skins by a million hours out in the tropical sun, white teeth that flashed with smiles and laughter, the perfect pair. The problem was that Mimi had spent time in Florida's Lowell Correctional Institute for Women, just north of Ocala, for five years and had walked off from a trustee work site one day and headed south. By the time she reached Key West she was reborn as Mimi Coffee with I.D. to back it up, and not a penny to her name. She used the only asset she had to survive, working up and down Duval hooking, rolling drunks, dodging the local cops, doing what she could to make it. One day she showed up at Tommy's dive shack with a few vacationers who wanted to snorkel off the Tortugas and hired out *The Island Girl* for the day. Tommy and Mimi hit it off and spent the day talking while the guests swam and goofed off in the water. After that, they were almost inseparable.

"Hey, Tommy, come on up. We need to talk," Jack called out.

"You're telling me," Tommy answered as he hopped onto the dock, wiping the sweat from his face and chest with an old towel.

"Hi, Jack," Mimi called out. "You here to rescue me from this hunky slave master?"

"Anytime you're ready, I'll come to your rescue, pretty woman."

"You guys knock it off. Mimi scrub. Jack inside."

The temp dropped about ten degrees once inside the shack, and they both exhaled in relief.

"Jack, we've really stepped in it this time. This could be a location changer, man," Tommy blurted out. "I shit you not, I'm talking major trouble."

"Ok, slow down, take it easy, and tell me what kind of trouble *we* are in."

"*Holy Crap*!" was all Jack could think to say after Tommy finished telling him about the drugs and the threat of not going along with the Cubans.

Jack had always believed that Cuban Americans were some of the most patriotic citizens the country had, but then, conversely, the Fidel Loyalist Cubans were just as furiously patriotic. The difference was that the rule of law differed greatly between the two countries, and the Fidel bunch believed murder was a viable concept in settling disputes.

"So, what are we going to do?" Tommy asked.

"*We?*"

"Yeah, *we*! You're the fire team leader, remember? You're supposed to know what to do at all times and watch out for all the peons. So what's the plan, do we rabbit, or do we go along with it?"

"Fuck Tommy, I don't know. But I'll tell you what I think — there is something else going on that could be part of *your* problem that will make it *our* problem," Jack said as he launched into the past twenty-four hours.

Tommy and Jack both came from similar backgrounds, where things growing up were lean and tough. Good times were when you had something to eat and you didn't have to move at the end of each month when the rent came due. Hanging out with friends was better than sitting around getting smacked by a drunk old man while watching your mom get the crap smacked out of her every night. Running with a tough crowd gave them the edge over normal kids growing up, where home life was all about them. For one thing, you weren't afraid to take it on the chin when somebody threw a punch. For another, you looked for any openings that would give you the advantage over a situation. If those two didn't work, you ran.

"It's got to be the same crew," Tommy declared after listening to the events of the last twenty-four hours. "Pointman just got caught in the middle and paid the price, but you can bet your ass that he told them everything he knew before they popped him."

"Yeah, that's my biggest worry right now. If these guys are the ones looking for the stolen drug money, *and* the same ones pushing for you to 'mule' their product, then you know they won't hesitate a second to pop us."

"Jack, this could work in our favor if we don't panic," Tommy said with that old street squint to his eyes, just like that day in the Kuwait vault. "What if we shoot over to the storage place and see what we got? If it's the money, I say we load up my truck and scoot on up to the mainland and disappear."

"It is tempting," Jack sighed. "Ten large ... very large, is nothing to just walk away from ... but Tommy, we can't, man. What about the bar ... hell, *The Island Girl*? You ready to walk away from her ... and Mimi?"

Jack was sitting on an old nail keg that served as a chair, trying to get a handle on what to do next. Tommy was leaning on the shop's display counter looking down at dive watches, knives, and regulators, his forehead creased in thought.

"We need to ride over to the storage locker and see what's inside before we can do anything. It might just be a key that Point found in one of the alleys. If he did take it off the dead guy over by the Coast Guard Base, it could still mean nothing. Maybe it's filled with household goods or crap the guy hauls around move to move," Jack said.

"Yeah, we should at least do that. Take a peek, and if it's nothing, then we only have the drug thing to worry about with Santos. I think we may have to just go along with what he says and run drugs and the money for a while until we can see a way out."

"… or get dead," Jack said.

—

Tommy pulled his pick-up truck onto the crushed-coral parking area of the Key West Storage lot, cut the motor, and they jumped out into the sweltering heat. Jack wasn't sure how they were going to get access to the space, but sometimes not having a plan was best. Just go in with a shoeshine and a smile.

"Hi there, fella, my name is Jack Marsh, I run the Sand Bar over on Duval."

"I know who you are, Mr. Marsh. I recognize you from that picture of you in the *Citizen News* a few months back. That sure was a brave thing you did, whipping the snot out of those boys fighting them dogs like that. Should a killed 'em, I say. What can I do for ya?"

Jack breathed a sigh of relief knowing they weren't going to have any trouble getting inside the storage area.

"Hey, just doing what I thought was right at the time. Anyone would have done the same," Jack said modestly.

Actually, he remembered very well what happened and it wasn't what the police and the news boys thought. A guy who lived over off Pearl in Old Town beat the hell out of one of Jack's waitresses one night after she got off work. He had followed her home, forced his way in, and tried to rape her. Fortunately, she got away from him, but not until her face had been smashed and a few teeth knocked out. The next day when Jack found out about it, he took the cricket bat he hid behind the bar to keep the place from being trashed when a few of the guys have had too much to drink. He rode his bicycle over to the guy's house, heard laughing and shouting coming from around back, and let himself through the gate. When he saw a circle of men shouting and yelling, and got a glimpse of two dogs, bloody and fighting in a dusty fur-ball, he lost it and just started swinging the cricket bat, hitting flesh and bone, cracking heads and yelling like a crazy man. Later on, when the cops showed up, there were seven guys laid out unconscious with head and face cuts, a few concussions and lots of abrasions. The *Citizen Newspaper* made a big deal out of how he had heard about the dog fights and went there on his own to stop them. The cops were happy with the bust and took credit for breaking up a dog-fighting ring in the city that lead to a similar bust up in Dade County. The girl recovered and moved back up to the mainland. The guy who tried to rape her was serving eighteen months for some cruelty to animals' law.

"Say listen, one of the guys who works for me has moved back up north and he wanted me to check on his storage unit. Says he has some old personal papers and letters that he wants to make sure haven't been damaged by all the humidity."

"Sure, what's the name and number," the manager said.

"Uh … the number is unit B-260, the … uh name is … uh Stanton, Charles Stanton. At least that's the name he gave me on his app when I hired him," I said.

"We ain't got no Stanton's on here under that unit. What other name did he go by?"

"Well, you know these people who just roll into town, you just never know what they're running from, or what their real name is, know what I mean?"

"Do I ever! I get so many names I could just as easily put down Tinker Bell. The name I got for that unit is Jones, John Jones. That's just what I'm saying."

They all laughed as the old man lead them outside and pointed down the lane to where the B units started. Jack thanked him and walked down the lane towards the unit. The two had their heads swiveling around like the bobble heads you see on car dashboards, bouncing all around. It wouldn't have taken much of a flashback to see themselves back on Kuwait City's narrow streets and alleys.

Tommy stood with his back to the pull door watching for snipers and muzzies to pop up at any second, while Jack bent down, inserted the key, popped the lock open, and then raised the door waist high.

"Here goes, buddy," Jack said and ducked inside.

The light was dim, but bright enough to see the back wall of the space filled with shrink wrapped bundles of … money? Jack took out a pocketknife and went to work on one of the bundles. Within seconds he was looking at banded stacks of fifty dollar bills. He cut through a second bundle … twenties, another bundle … hundreds.

"Oh, my God, are we in deep shit!" Jack said softly.

"Jack, what the fuck, what's in there?" Tommy called out, sticking his head under the opening. "Holy crap! Is that what I think it is?" he said, and came in the rest of the way.

They opened a few more bundles and found that the denominations were twenties, fifties, or hundreds, nothing smaller.

"I think I'm getting a boner," Tommy joked. "Look at all this … this … cash!"

"Tommy, this is big trouble," Jack said, not able to take his eyes off the wall of money in front of him.

Jack's mind was racing with possibilities, opportunities, and things to buy — escape. This was the lottery come true. His mind was off on a shopaholic's euphoric buying spree; cars, boats, women, travel … women. He was even thinking of buying his ex's jewels back and returning them to her. That thought brought him back to the real world.

"Let's get the hell out of here, now," Jack said.

"What are you talking about? We ain't going anywhere without the money. You stay here, I'll bring the truck around," Tommy said and turned to go.

"Hold on, not so fast, Tommy. We need to think."

An hour later, they pulled out of the storage lot and headed back to the dive shop. Before leaving, they rented the space across the alley from B-260, bagged all the bundles in large green leaf bags, and moved them across the alley to B-261. They pulled an old sofa and a pee-stained mattress from the dumpster and put them inside the old unit, wiped their prints off everything, and locked it up. They also took two bundles of hundreds for the inconvenience of having to work in all that heat and humidity. It was easy to justify keeping the money for themselves because it was dirty money — and anyways, it wasn't like stealing. They were just taking it away from bad men and not hurting anyone. Besides, if the feds got their hands on it, it would disappear down some Washington drain anyway, so it might as well go for a good cause.

Chapter 5

The Monroe County Sheriff's complex was a no-frills building located on Stock Island behind the Key West Country Club, set back off the beaten path from Highway 1 which led into Key West. Lighting in the parking lot was minimal at night to save on energy and to stay in line with the new Sheriff's directive, one of many of the new boss's pet projects to cut costs on non-essentials and low return expenses. Another budget item Sheriff Perry focused on was shift length and overtime. Since winning by a landslide in the last election on a platform of cutting department costs and zero tolerance on crime, he had held true to his campaign promises and was quickly despised by the rank and file. The most significant change was going from three eight-hour shifts to two twelve-hour shifts and the doubling up of workload and special assignments.

One of those special assignments was created as a result of the two gang-style murders in the last thirty-six hours. The Sheriff saw the murders as a personal attack on his commitment to cleaning up Key West and wasn't going to stand for it. What was also becoming apparent to the troops was that the new Sheriff liked to spread risk and failure around, with successes spotlighted back on him.

At 21:00 hours the Gang Task Force held its first briefing, with the Sheriff presiding, Lt. Mathers as the task force head, Sgt. Bill Short second, and three rookies new to the department made up the balance of the team. Surprisingly, Sheriff Perry had invited Jim Olsen of the DEA to join in on the briefing. Agent Olsen worked out of the DEA's Miami office, which covered Miami-Dade and Monroe Counties, an area that accounted for thirty-percent of all drugs entering the country, and millions in cash leaving the country annually.

"We all know why we're here," Sheriff Perry started out, "I have some caballeros thinking that they can come riding in here and shoot the place up like this was the OK Corral. I remember when Key West was seen as a stopover for every mule and drug runner coming up from the south where they could hide, take a crap, and move on. *It's not going to happen!* Those days are gone, gentlemen!" He yelled and pounded the table.

"Now you listen to me, and you listen good. In five days, I want the hides of whoever did these killings hung from the Keys greeting sign in Florida City, so every swinging dick that comes down Highway 1 will know I don't put up with gunplay in my territory. Is that clear?"

"Sir, I would like to have further clarification on your definition of *hides,*" one of the young deputies asked.

"Hides, skins, furs, fillets … dimwit! What do you think I mean?" The Sheriff said, face beet-red in anger. "Now, you limp dicks figure out how you're going to do it and get on it. Everything is on the table. You are to do whatever it takes to bring good order and discipline back into Monroe County. I'll run interference for you and keep other agencies off your back. Just don't be caught doing anything out of line on some damn television camera. If that happens, I won't be able to protect you," he said and stood to go. "Now, get on it. You now have four days, twenty-three hours … and whatever." At the door, he turned and pointed at Agent Olsen, "See me in my office before you leave, Jim."

The team sat in silence looking at the door the Sheriff had just banged shut. It took several moments for air to fill the room again and sighs could be heard coming from the rookies down at the end of the table.

'Nice guy," Agent Olsen said, pointing his chin towards the door. "He always that friendly?"

"Well, he's new, you know, still feeling his way," Lt. Mathers said to hide his embarrassment at the way his boss acted in front of the troops. "He'll settle down once he sees how things work around here."

Bill Short shook his head in disgust, "We had his kind in the Rangers. Just as soon get the troops killed so he can get a medal."

"Cool it, Sergeant," Lt. Mathers said. "Now, let's get down to the business at hand. Word back from the National Data Base shows our dead unknown as one Umberto Cruz from Miami, a member of the *Calle Ocho* Gang, also known as the Eighth Street Gang, or, in Little Havana, as the 8s. Big on narcotics, steal anything not nailed down, murder for hire, or fun. Mean little shits, and there's a lot of them, ranging from early teens to mid-thirties."

"Let me step in just for a second, Loot," Agent Olsen said. "We know these mutts, and they are worse than what your Lieutenant says. Word is that they are getting into the big leagues, pulling cocaine up through Cuba, washing money back down the same pipe. Their founder is one of the old

Mariel boatlift people who came across in 1980 with his dad when he was a little boy of five or so. His name is Pascal Gomez, but calls himself the Condor. He has high-placed ties back in Cuba with Fidel's government and the drugs that pass through there heading north to the U.S. and the money going back down south. Fidel is believed to take a few percent of every shipment going both ways. Now he wants to get in on the profitable gun running business. I have a couple of my guys working deep in with the gang on that angle and we're hearing that things are moving forward. Meanwhile, Gomez is running into trouble getting his money out of the U.S. It's rumored that he's sitting on a half-billion dollars in cash somewhere around Miami with more coming in every day from up north. He's desperate to get a new pipeline going to undo the logjam. Tonight's murders could be tied to that activity."

"That's some scary stuff, Lieutenant," one of the rookies spoke up. "How are five of us going to bring down a gang like that?"

"First off, we're not bringing down the gang. We're looking for the murderer of two men here in the county. If the murderer is tied to this Condor's gang, the chances are we'll never find him. But we're sure as hell going to try, and we're going to do it within the rule of law ... no hides hanging from fences, clear?" Lt. Mathers said.

"I'm sure that's why the Sheriff brought me in on this. If you men step into some shit, we'll be here to back you up," Agent Olsen added confidently.

At a quarter of two in the morning, Agent Olsen pulled into the big circular drive of the Gomez mansion off Harbor Drive on Key Biscayne. Olsen hated coming here, even in the middle of the night, on the off chance that some other agency had the place under surveillance. It didn't bother him that he was a sell-out to one of the cruelest and most ruthless thugs to ever come out of Little Havana, or that he had corrupted his own team of agents to turn against their oath of allegiance to the department. What bugged him was that he wasn't going to hit his goal of five million bucks before his transfer to D.C. next month. He had received his papers from the director himself, stating that he was being promoted and reassigned back to headquarters for the duration of his career.

Tonight was going to be especially dangerous for him. He would have to be very careful about how he acted and what he said. The ten million dollars that he and his men helped steal from Gomez's money crew four days ago had disappeared and hadn't been found yet; money that had been destined for a pick-up out in the Straits two nights ago. Word on the street was that Gomez was frantic about the theft because it was his head on the chopping block if he didn't make it up. The whole plan had turned to crap when that asshole, Umberto Cruz, double crossed him and hid the money somewhere in Key West for himself. Then that fucking drugged-out Vietnam dirt bag had witnessed them kill Umberto in the old Navy container yard. The goofball had stripped Umberto's body of everything after they had pulled out in a panic. Finding the dirt bag was no problem, but trying to get information out of him was a different story. The only thing they got out of the old shit before he died was that someone named Black Alice would put a curse on them and Captain Jack Marsh would send a patrol out to bring his body back. Crazy old fucker.

A shadowy figure with an M16 stepped out from behind a clump of Coconut palms and approached Olsen.

"Good evening, Mr. Smith," the guard said once he was sure who the visitor was. He knew that wasn't the man's real name, and he really didn't care what it was. His job was to protect *El Condor*, and to kill anyone who tried to get by him — period.

"Hi, I think the Jefe is waiting for me."

"Si, he said for me to let you in immediately."

The house was a huge two-story Spanish hacienda-themed mansion with tropical gardens, palms, and flowers around the two-acre compound that always gave off a delicious smell of the tropics. To Olsen, the inside of the house was over-stuffed with furniture, paintings, wall-murals, potpourri, old framed photos of long dead Cuban patriarchs, and clutter. The place was permeated with the burnt smell of plantains, black beans, and pork, and something else Olsen could never put his finger on. Gomez was in the huge den watching a variety show on the TeleMundo channel, sitting in his boxer shorts, smoking a cigar with a bare-bosomed woman cuddled up close in a double-sized recliner.

"Mr. Smith, welcome. Come join us. We are about to find out which of tonight's singers will win the grand prize. Marta says it will be the pretty boy with the tight pants. I say it will be the little chica singing Ave Maria. Come sit."

Olsen noticed that three men sat off in a corner playing dominos, slapping them down loudly, intent on the game, but always with a wary eye on their master. The slightest indication of harm to the Condor and these men would spring into action. While the last few minutes of the variety show wound down, Olsen took in his surroundings with disgust. While he never regretted going rogue, and had no qualms about the money he was getting from illegal activities, he only felt bad that he had to take this route in the first place. The Agency was so top heavy with appointees, friends of friends and relatives that a hard-working field agent would never make it to the top. He also consoled himself with the knowledge that there were agents all over the DEA who were taking kickbacks, selling department information, and dealing in narcotics. For the right price, any agent could be turned.

"Via Chica," Pascal said to his chair mate with a slap to her butt. "Ok, Jim let us talk business, the hour is late, and I have had a busy day. What have you learned of my money that was stolen from under my nose by filthy traitors?" Gomez said in a deadly tone, eyes locked like a viper's, ready to strike.

"As of this minute, Jefe, I don't know. I have my men spread out all over the Keys looking for any clue, but nothing so far. As I reported to you last night, we interrogated Umberto before he ... died, to find out if he was involved with the thieves, but he didn't tell us anything. Another man, who my agents discovered, proved to be a dead end with nothing to tell us."

"*Silence!* I do not want to hear about your failures, Olsen. I want results. Do you not understand the situation? There are ten million dollars ... *Dias Mellones, Señor,* stolen from me, money that I owe to the Sanchez Cartel. Señor Sanchez himself has given me until tomorrow night to make the money appear. Do you think I can make ten million dollars appear if I snap my fingers?" Gomez yelled loudly, spittle showering Olsen's face.

Olsen saw that Gomez's rage was building to a deadly level and that this was a critical moment to his survival.

"Jefe, please let me finish. I was saying that even though we have interrogated two men, there are still others who we have yet to talk with. I am a member of the Sheriff's special task force and will hear of any news before anyone else does and will be the first to speak with the suspects. I also have the names of two people obtained from the last man we talked to ..."

"Give me the names. Are they my people?"

"No, Jefe, they are in Key West. An island woman named Black Alice and a man, Jack Marsh. I am going to scoop these two up and have a talk with them as soon as I leave here, Jefe."

Gomez took the soggy cigar stub out of his mouth and pointed it at Olsen, "The people I am dealing with have made it very clear to me that if I do not deliver their money by tomorrow night, I will be dead by morning of the next day. *Desayuno con pesci* — I will have breakfast with the fishes, Señor, and you will be with me. Do you understand, Señor Olsen?"

"Yeah, I understand," Olsen said, getting steamed up at this fat piñata and his constant threats. "Life's a risk, Gomez, save your threats for the meatheads over there. Without me watching your back you wouldn't be sitting here watching some stupid fucking talent show," Olsen said gruffly. "As long as we're on the subject, I want a bigger payday starting …"

"*A bigger payday*! You are lucky that I have not had you killed. There will be no bigger payday, you cockroach! You do not come into my house and try to steal from me!" the Condor yelled, snapping his fingers loudly.

Within a nano-second the three domino players were on top of Olsen, swinging punches. Olsen flinched, but not soon enough to duck the big ham-sized fist that landed on his jaw, and another quick slam to the chest that knocked the wind out of him.

"You Putá! I pay you to do as I say. You mean nothing to me, filthy piece of shit! I tell you what you get, you get nothing, do you hear me? *Nada!* You show me no respect in front of my loyal soldiers and make fun of me behind my back. So I will tell you, gringo, you will work for me for nothing. If you try and screw with me, I will kill your wife and your children while you watch, then I will kill you. You think this is a game, Señor? No, this is no game. You are not even a player in this game, but now you have a stake in it — *your life,*" the Condor said and spit on Olsen. "Take him outside and beat him. Don't kill him, just hurt him."

Chapter 6

Jack smelled coffee as he bounced down the stairs two at a time, humming a song that had been running through his mind all morning like a broken record, *Every time it rains, it rains ...* over and over. Jack hadn't felt this good in months, he was sitting on a hundred large in the safe, had five-million and change as his share of the loot stashed in the rental space, and he lived in Key West. *Pennies from heaven ...*

"Good morning, Cookie," Jack sang out as he whizzed through the kitchen. "Good morning, Lamont."

"Yo, Mr. Jack. What're you so happy about this morning? Get lucky last night?" Lamont asked with a puzzled look on his face.

"Something better, my man. I had a dream I was coming into some big bucks and that I was going to share it with all my friends," he said.

"Hot damn! We're rich!" Lamont sang out.

"I said my *friends*, not my *humps*. Get to work on those tables, we have customers waiting."

"*Humps*! Ain't that some shit!" Lamont said, wagging his head and getting back to placing chairs around tables.

Jack opened the receipt drawer where he kept all papers, invoices, deposits, and miscellaneous stuff that it takes to run a business, and his good mood crashed. He stood with his hand on the drawer looking down at Point's pistol, a grim reminder that trouble was still heavy in the air and there was still a murderer on the loose who had killed twice for the money they swiped. A chill ran up his back. He had the feeling eyes were watching him. He reached in the drawer to pick up the pistol —

"Hey, Jacky, come over here."

"Sure thing, Mr. C," he called out, letting the fear wash away.

"Sit and take a coffee with me," Mr. Cona said, pointing to a chair across from him.

"Sure, let me grab the coffee first," he said and hustled over to get two espressos cooking. "Lamont, bring those over when they're ready."

"So, Jacky, you doing ok? Anything bothering you? Anything I can do for you?"

"No Mr. C, I'm fine. Can't think of a thing I need, but I appreciate the offer."

"Too bad you ain't Italian. I know it's not your fault. We got to deal with what God gave us, right, Jack?"

"I agree all the way. Yes sir, couldn't have said it better myself."

"One minute you're up, the next you're down. Up and down, that's what life is, like a bunch of fucking speed bumps. Take that Castro for instance. One minute he's up, the next he's down. You get to be as old as him and you start making mistakes, let your guard down and … *Bam*! Somebody nails ya between the eyes. You follow me, Jack?"

"Yes sir, life's a bitch."

"I think there's a lot of folks would be glad to see Fidel go the way that shit bird Bobby Kennedy did, don't you think?"

"I guess, Mr. C. That was way before my time."

"Time don't mean anything. A man breaks his word it's broken forever. A man breaks his word or doesn't keep his commitments, then what kind of man is that?"

"A dead man, Mr. C.?"

"See, Junior? I told you this Jacky is smart, even if he is an Irish," Mr. C said as he patted Jack on the cheek.

"Come closer," Mr. C said as he bent forward over the table.

"Tonight, you and your friend with the boat, Tommy Hicks, are going to meet up with some people out in the stream, capiche?" He paused to look around for eavesdroppers, "Two things are going to happen. My friends will be on Tommy Hicks's boat with some special merchandise, and when the two boats meet and tie up, my guys are going to move the merchandise and some bags of equipment over to the Cuban boat. Next, some drugs will be moved from the Cuban boat and will be loaded on board your friend's boat to bring back here. I know this may be confusing for you, so ask questions. You want me to repeat it?"

"Uh, Mr. Cona, why do you want to involve me and my friend in this … uh heist? We don't know anything about how this stuff is done. We could screw it up and worse, get your men killed … or us."

"You think this is easy? Pull off a job like this when you got every outfit in the country following what's happening tonight? Christ, Jacky, you and that Hicks meathead are the only ones in this that don't know what's at stake. You got that turncoat Cuban calls himself El Condor trying to be a big shot and run with the spic cartels. He is worse than Fidel. He kills his own people just for fun. Then the DEA mutts are so far up El Condor's ass that they stole his weekly wash and the pezzonovante don't even know it. Well, tonight the chickens come home, Jacky. My family is making its move. We're taking Gomez and his whole Cuban Calle Ocho gang out of the drug trade. This time tomorrow, the Key West route belongs to the Cona family."

"Fuck, Mr. C. There is no way I want to be involved in any of this at all. I got a little business here and I'm happy. I'm not trying to be rich or anything like that. Sure, I play poker a couple of times a month, but I go to church sometimes, too. I'm not a gangster. Yeah, I'll run a hustle every now and then, but nothing that's going to cost me my life," Jack blathered as his mind was running on hyper speed to find a way out of this mess he and Tommy were in.

"Junior, I take back what I said. I don't think he understands what I'm saying," Mr. C. said. "Jacky, listen to me. You think I like being down here in this shithole? You think I like the sun and the heat? No, I hate it. Every day I say this, I hate it, but I have a duty, so I stay. You know what my duty is, Jacky? I'll tell you. My duty is to obey orders. Not to cry about it or complain about it, just obey it. My orders are to set up a major route to move drugs up from Cuba to Key West and equipment back down through Key West to Cuba. The time is now. We have waited and watched, and put big money in a lot of officials' hands for this moment, the political fix is in place and now the day is here. This is just a small part of a much bigger plan. The only reason you and Hicks are involved is because Colonel Miguel Santos has personally spent many hours developing the weekly black market run with Mr. Hicks. Meanwhile, it took much time and effort for him to betray and kill men inside El Presidenté's secret drug operation. Now Colonel Santos has the trust of Fidel and heads the drug operation, while Castro sits back and burns holes in his lungs with those cheap Havana cigars. So, we need Hicks and his boat one last time to make the drop off of some very special equipment, and to steal Gomez's last load of drugs." Old man Cona wheezed a few times, sat back to catch his breath, then sat forward and whispered.

"Jacky, we are going to kill Castro and his little brother and put in a new government that is amenable to our business. Colonel Santos is that man. Now do you understand? It's been three generations of Cubans since Batista ran the country. The people are worse off now than ever, no food, no conveniences, no nothing. Me and my friends are going to bring Cuba back to life. We're going to come back so strong that the Cuban people in Miami will be pleading to go back." Mr. C paused and took a slurp of his coffee.

"Do you know that there are people who will kill you just for knowing what I just told you? So, Mr. Big Shot Bar

Owner, now you are going to be part of history, whether you want to be or not. If you choose not to help then you will simply become a casualty, your choice."

"I'm fucked!" Jack answered, thinking life with Sophie wouldn't be so bad about now, maybe back up in Georgia or Kentucky in the mountains, out of sight. He just needed to give it a chance is all.

"Yeah my friend, you are fucked if you don't do like you're told. Capiche, Jacky? Then when this is over, you can visit me in Havana and we'll laugh about all this. Maybe I'll let you open a bar for the tourists."

"Mr. C …"

"Uh uh, don't say it, Jacky, you say the wrong thing and I might have to ask Junior to have a private talk with you. Come close," Mr. C said. "You play ball with me, when this is over I'll give you twenty cents on the dollar for the money you got stashed …"

"But! *What money?*" Jack gasped feeling like he had just been slapped.

"Ha-ha! Oh boy, Junior, this Mick thinks he's dealing with amateurs," the old man laughed, sitting back slapping his knee. "Of course I know about the money. My boys have been following it since that schlemiel Olsen stole it from Gomez. Hell, we were going to steal it before Olsen made his move but that joker beat us to it. Then all the killing and the police all around, we just sat on it. It's safe where it is for now, and to show my gratitude for helping out on this I'll pay you top return on the wash."

"Mr. C I ... uh ... I just don't know what to say."

"So, what's to say, Jacky? Your tit's in a wringer and I'm holding the crank. You'll come out of this, just do as you're told." The Mafia Don said and snapped his fingers. Junior quickly pulled the Don's chair out and brushed him off with his kerchief.

"And, Jacky, from now on I want your boy Lamont to make the espresso. He makes it like an Italian. Ok?"

Chapter 7

Jack sat frozen in his chair as the old Mafia Don walked out holding on to Junior's arm for support. His mind was trying to digest everything the Don had told him, but the bottom line was that he and Tommy were expected to go out on the Straits tonight with some men they didn't know, along with a load of some kind of merchandise, and pass it to Colonel Santos, who, until now, Jack thought was a lowly Navy Commandant doing coastal patrol, making a few extra bucks running black market goods through his partner, Tommy Hicks. Now it seems that Miguel Santos is going to be the next el Presidente of Cuba if Mr. Cona has his way. The scope of what the Don was doing was unbelievable, that is unless he had the backing of the U.S. government to pull it off. If the Feds said hands-off, then there was no way the Mafia could do something this big on their own. It was just too big of an operation. All this was way above Jack's pay grade and he didn't want any part of it. But the news about this Gomez drug lord in Miami, who was going to get whacked by the Don's people today or tonight, was lighting off claymores in his mind. Jack had ten million dollars of the man's money that had been stolen by some rogue DEA agent, then somehow the agent lost the money. Pointman had stumbled into the picture and was tortured for any information he may have had regarding the money. If Point had talked while being cut up, then the agent could be on to Jack at this very moment.

How much more can this get screwed up? The Don waltzes in and says he's going to assassinate Castro, and if I go along with him on the delivery and pickup tonight, he'll pay me twenty cents on the dollar ... of my money! Well, mine for now. Jack flipped open his cell phone and called Tommy.

"Island Divers," Mimi answered in her soft sexy voice.

"Mimi, it's me Jack. I need to talk with Tommy, chop-chop."

"Hi Jack. Tommy's out front talking to some guy says he's with the DEA. This guy looks like he had a serious argument with a gorilla or something big."

"Mimi, get Tommy's attention and tell him that Smedley is on the line, it's important," Jack said. Smedley was a name used in the Marines to identify a recruit who screwed up. It would alert Tommy to trouble.

"I'll try, hold on."

A few moments went by, "Yeah Smedley, what's up?"

"Tommy, that DEA guy is probably the guy who killed Point. Don't tell him nothing, shine him on, get rid of him. The shit has hit the fan and we need to talk ASAP, partner."

"Yeah … uh, Smedley, I think I get your drift here," Tommy said, then dropped his voice to a whisper. "He's asking if I know where you are and if I've seen you in the last few days. I told him that, the last I heard, you were up on the mainland to buy some bar equipment and should be back by the end of the week. He's also asking about Black Alice."

"Black Alice? That's the second time I've heard her name in the last two days. What does she have to do with all this?" Jack asked. "Listen, don't tell that guy anything. I'm shooting over to see Black Alice and find out what she knows. You get rid of that guy. Whatever you do, don't go anywhere with him.

"Got it," Tommy said and hung up.

Jack popped his cell closed and hurried over to the bar, pulled the receipt drawer open, and stuck the pistol in his waistband.

"Whoa, big fella, where you going with that popgun?" Coco asked.

"When was the last time you saw Black Alice?"

"Black Alice? Jack what are you into? Stay away from that woman, she'll put a spell on you and steal your mind," Coco said, alarmed. Black Alice was the Island's "voodoo mistress," as she liked to call herself. Many of the locals went to her for advice and counseling. It was rumored that she practiced the darker side of the witchcraft to cast out demons and bad spirits — for a price.

"Don't worry, I don't believe in all that hoodoo doo doo stuff. I need to talk to her about something Pointman may have said to her."

Coco made a quick sign of the cross, "Don't make fun, Jack. Some people say there's more people that believe in voodoo than there are Catholics. I know some of the things she does is spooky, but she does make weird things happen."

———

Jack jumped in a pedal-cab outside the Sand Bar and told the guy where he wanted to go.

"I'll take you as far as Truman and drop you off, but I won't take you all the way in," the young guy pedaling the three-wheeler said.

Jack wasn't surprised. Many of the residents stayed away from that end of town because of the drugs, and the risk of being rolled or beat up for your wallet or watch. It was an area best avoided unless you had business there. Several juke joints were scattered around that stayed open all night, with singers belting out their sorrowful Mississippi style blues, as the audience threw down shots of rye and gin. Jack never felt uncomfortable going in these places when he just wanted to get away and listen to some good blues. Several times he had hired juke bands to play his place when Jimmy Boofey disappeared for a few days.

Jack hopped off the pedal-cab, gave the kid a couple of bucks for the ride and walked down an alley leading off Duval. Two blocks over, he stepped into a joint called Ike's, named after its owner, bartender, bouncer, and conversationalist.

"My man, Jack. Z'up Bro? What brings Duval royalty down here to the projects?" Ike said, coming around the bar to shake Jack's hand. The room was icy cold and smelled of booze, cigarettes and stale urine. Jack could feel others in the room, but his eyes were still pinpricks from the tropical sun outside.

"Hey, Ike, glad to see you," Jack said, as Ike squeezed his hand in a vice-grip hold. "I'm looking for somebody, but I don't know exactly where she lives."

"You looking for a woman, Jack? What kind? I can fix you up without you being out in that hot sun. What you want: Puerto Rican chick, Cuban, Jamaican, maybe something else …?"

"I'm looking for Black Alice …"

"Black Alice! What business you got with Black Alice, Jack? She ain't got nothing for you."

"I need to talk to her about a mutual friend who was killed the other night. The day he died, he mentioned her name to me and I need to warn her that she may be in trouble with the people who killed our friend."

"You talking about that crazy homeless dude, Pointman? That man used to sleep in her yard at times, with all those chickens she keeps, come out the next morning smelling something awful. Black Alice make him wash off out of that rain barrel of water before letting him inside."

"Yeah, I'm talking Pointman. His killers beat him hard before they shot him, trying to get information they thought he had."

"Word on the corner is that Gomez lost a lot of money somewhere around here and has some shooters flying up and down Highway 1 looking for it," Ike said, then bent in close to Jack. "Now I don't know for sure, and I can't say if it's true, but a man told me that the new Sheriff is working with Gomez to find that money, and if he finds the dude who stole it, his orders from El Condor are to bring the person to him, alive."

"How reliable is your friend?" Jack asked, feeling sick to his stomach.

Ike looked closely at Jack's pale face and stepped back, alarmed at what he thought he saw, "What you know about all this, Jack? Something ain't coming together here in my mind. I hope you ain't involved in any of this, are you?"

"Nah," Jack recovered his composure. "I'm just following up on what I heard about Black Alice being drawn into Point's murder somehow that's all, and I need to warn her that a man is coming around to see her who she shouldn't see."

"What man? Are you saying somebody is going to try and hurt Black Alice?"

"I don't know for sure what is going on, but I think she needs to be warned. The guy is a DEA agent but I think he's gone bad and is probably the one who stole the Condor's money. Now he's trying to cover his tracks."

Ike motioned to a man sitting at the other end of the bar to come to him. Once the man hopped off his bar stool, Jack saw that he wasn't any taller than the bar itself, and emaciated. His big ears held up a too-large *DOLPHINS* cap.

"S'cuse me, Jack, but I need to talk to Skinny for a minute," he said and began speaking rapidly in Creole to the man. Ike patted Skinny on the shoulder as he talked for a couple of minutes, then Skinny abruptly turned and hurried out the door without saying a word.

"Jack, you go on back up to your end of town. We're going to see to it that Black Alice is safe. Nobody's coming down here to do anything unless we say so. You go on and I'll let you know if anything comes up," Ike said as he walked Jack to the door. "Black Alice is special to us, Jack. She's sort of like our own saint, but more magical than those other saints in the white church. Besides, she don't speak English, only Creole, so no need you going over there to talk to her. She won't have a clue what you're talking about ... and Jack, watch yourself."

Jack's mind was blowing through all the different scenarios of what could happen to him if he made any mistakes or tripped up somehow over the next twenty-four hours. The thought of having the Sheriff hunting him, along with the DEA agent, Gomez's gun monkeys, and Don Cona squeezing his cajones made Jack want to scoot over to the airport and fly away. So far, two people were dead, Pointman and the DEA snitch — how many more lives were on the line? It seemed like guns were pointed at each other around a circle waiting for the first person to trip up. If the old Don was right, Gomez should be off the board sometime today. That would slow the Sheriff down and put the DEA agent in a better position to look for the money without anyone on his butt to kill him. As Jack mulled all this over, a plan started to formulate in his old devious mind that could get them out of the gun sights and still let them keep the money.

Jack called Tommy and talked with him for a few minutes, telling him what he wanted to do and how they were going to do it. He then copied Agent Olsen's cell number on his palm with a ballpoint.

"Are you sure about this, Jack?" Tommy asked. "If this gets fucked up, we're dead."

"No, I'm not sure, but we just can't wait around for someone to pop our asses, can we? We need to go on the offensive," Jack said and snapped his cell phone closed.

Thirty minutes later, as Tommy and Jack were loading up the sacks of money from the storage room into the back of Tommy's pick up, Agent Olsen pulled in at an angle, parked, and got out. Olsen held a big chrome plated pistol at his side as he cautiously approached the two men.

"Well, Tommy, it was smart of you to contact your partner and tell him to call me. This could have gone real bad for both of you," Agent Olsen said through swollen lips from the beating he had received by Gomez's mutts.

"Gosh, Agent Olsen, we didn't understand what we had gotten into. But now, thank God, you're here to take this off our hands," Jack said contritely.

"Well, we still have a little problem we have to discuss. Let's step inside the space out of this sun," Olsen said motioning with his pistol while taking a quick look over his shoulder.

"Sure," Tommy said, backing into the room followed by Jack and then Olsen.

As soon as Olsen stepped inside, Tommy poked him in the chest with a Taser, giving him an electroshock that knocked him to his knees, then onto his face. Olsen lost all muscular control and was jerking uncontrollably. His eyes rolled back in his head, tongue lolling. Jack scooped up the pistol and stuck it into his waistband, then tossed the last three bags of money into the bed of the pickup. Tommy got busy cuffing Olsen's hands and feet with zip strips, then covered his mouth and eyes with duct tape wound tight around his head. He pulled a watch cap down over Olsen's face and stepped back to admire his work.

"Grab his feet, let's get him in the pickup before he comes out of it," Jack said, grabbing Olsen's shoulders.

Tommy took a quick look outside and grabbed the feet. Within seconds, Olsen was on the back floorboard of the crew cab.

"Jack, give me one of those pistols. You're going to shoot your pecker off carrying guns around like that."

Jack handed him Olsen's big .45 automatic, then placed the pistol he had been carrying on the front seat. As Tommy threw a tarp over the bed of the pickup and cinched it down,

Jack cranked up the plain-wrap police car Olsen had been driving and backed it into the storage space once Tommy had backed out of the way. Jack shut the car down, careful to turn off the police radio and to wipe his fingerprints down as he got out. Jack grabbed a .12-gauge street sweeper shotgun from the backseat and a case of road flares from the floorboard, tossed them in the pickup, and closed and locked the storage room door.

"Don't do anything wrong, Tommy. This would not be a good time to be stopped for speeding," Jack said, as he nervously looked around.

Olsen was moaning but had stopped shaking.

"You think he has any permanent damage?" Jack asked.

"Nah, he'll be all right. If we have to, we can pop him a few more times before he has any mental issues."

"What kind of issues? We don't want to kill the man."

"Mostly neuromuscular problems, the shakes, hallucinations, stuff like that. We had to study all that at the Sheriff's Academy. Some cop up in Miami held his Taser against a crackhead for a minute and the kid went into seizures and died. The cop got tried for murder and took a ten-year bounce, but a few pops won't hurt long-term"

Tommy drove down the narrow backstreets, hung a right on Amelia, then parked in front of Ike's. Ike and Skinny had been waiting for them and came out quickly when Tommy tapped the horn.

"Is this the man looking for Black Alice?" Ike asked, opening the crew door and leaning in.

"Yeah, this is him. He had a big .45 in his hand thinking he was going to cap us until Tommy zapped him with a Taser that made him change his mind."

"Well, let's get him around back before somebody takes a notice to us," Ike said.

While the three others hustled Olsen down a side footpath, Jack pulled one of the green bags out of the truck bed and threw it over his shoulder, following them around back. Olsen was tossed in a corner of a storage shed half filled with broken barstools, neon beer signs, and cases of empty booze bottles.

"He'll be ok back here. I'll put Tiny on him to make sure he don't try and get out," Ike said and whistled for Tiny. A big German shepherd nosed the back door of the bar open and trotted over to the shed.

"Meet Tiny. He knows fifty ways to kill a man, but mostly he just bites and holds on," Ike joked as he patted the dog's head. Ike took him inside the shed, pointed at Olsen, and gave him a verbal command. Tiny immediately dropped down on his belly and stared at Olsen.

"On the phone I said I would slip you a little something for helping me out on this," Jack said as he hefted the bag, passing it over to Ike. "All of us local businessmen need to stick together, don't we? Kind of share the wealth?" Jack said with a huge smile.

Ike's head snapped back after a quick look inside, "Oh my, what we got here?" he said taking a longer look. "There ain't nothing but sweet honeybees inside here, mmm mm, they sure are pretty, Jack. How you want me to kill this man — fried, baked, or broiled?"

Jack laughed, "No killing, sit on him until this time tomorrow. If you don't hear back from me by then, zap him a couple of times and have someone drop him somewhere up in Miami with nothing but his pants on," Jack said, and motioned for Tommy to give Ike the Taser.

Ike hefted the Taser in his big hand and motioned for Skinny to come closer. "Come here, Skinny, let's see if you got any lead in that pencil stub you're always bragging about," Ike said as Skinny backpedaled out of reach.

"Uh-uh, Ike, you stay away from me with that thing. I don't need no exterior appliances to help me out. The ladies enjoy me just fine," Skinny said in a high voice.

Chapter 8

Tommy had just finished with the last bolt on the decompression chamber's hatch when Sergeant Bill Short drove up in his squad car. Jack and Tommy had crammed most of the bags of money into the chamber thinking it would be the last place anyone would look for the cash. Two bags were still sitting beside the ten-foot cylinder that they couldn't cram in.

"Damn, Tommy, you still screwing around with that old chamber? It's never going to work. Why do you suppose the Navy sold it for salvage?" Short asked. "I know for sure I'll never let you put me in it. I would rather take my chances with the bends than a sure death in that rusty tube."

"We were just talking about you, Bill," Jack said. "Tommy thought for sure we could get you inside to try it out. He's put on all new gaskets, a brand new vacuum pump, the works. Take that cop gear off and hop in."

"No friggin' way, Jack. Besides, I'm on duty."

"What's the latest on Pointman's murder? Any breaks in the case?" Jack asked innocently.

"Lot of stuff going on, but no one person we can collar yet. Someone tried to blow up Gomez while he sat at one of those curbside Cuban cafés in Miami's Little Havana today. Killed a couple of his body guards and wounded a few other customers, but El Condor got away with a few cuts and scratches," Bill said.

Jack reached down, hefted up one of the money bags and started for the other when Bill reached down and beat him to it.

"Here let me help you with that," Bill said. "Damn its heavy, what the hell is inside here?" As he started to open it up, Tommy snatched it out of Bill's hand.

"Just paper towels soaked in vomit from the last guy to use the chamber. It was caked on and we had to scrub hard to get it off. It was nasty" Tommy said convincingly.

"Whatever," Bill said, and continued on. "Lt. Mathers thinks it was an attempt by the cartel to get rid of Gomez because of him losing the week's drug money."

"Drug money?" Jack asked innocently.

"Yeah, this is what this is all about, didn't you know? I thought I told you about how the two murders are tied to El Condor's gang. Someone stole the weekly wash between Miami and here, and now every gun in South Florida is looking for it. Shooters are pouring into the Keys by the carload hoping to find it. The Sheriff has a road block set up at the eighteen-mile stretch leading into Key Largo to stop any suspicious people from coming down," Billy said as he held open the dumpster lid while Jack and Tommy carefully tossed the money bags in.

"Well, I heard rumors, but I had no idea about all the guns heading to Key West. What are you guys doing locally?"

"The Sheriff has a DEA agent working with us on the team, but hell, he disappeared right after our first meeting last night and we haven't heard anything from him since. Lt. Mathers says that he didn't want the guy involved anyway because of rumors about him being on the Condor's payroll."

"How's the new Sheriff to work for, Billy?" Tommy asked.

"He's an asshole. None of us can figure him out. One day he says one thing, the next it's something else. Lt. Mathers doesn't trust him after he was spotted at the Seven Mile Grill up in Marathon having a drink with one of the Condor's bagmen. He has us giving him updates every hour, asking where we are on our investigation, what have we found out, who we have talked to. It's driving the Lieutenant nuts."

"Look, I can't stand around all day being seen talking to the law. Besides, I have to gas up *The Girl*, big night tonight," Tommy said.

"Oh yeah, what's up tonight?" Bill asked.

"Uh … group night dive. I'm taking some guys out to the Tortugas for an all- nighter."

"Hey, I get off at five. How about me coming along?" Bill said.

"No can do, Billy, not tonight. I have a full boat. I'm not even taking Mimi on this one."

"What about you, Jack? Want to go after some bonefish out on the flats?"

"Not tonight, Bill. I have a date with my accountant, maybe later in the week."

"Well, fuck you guys. I was just kidding anyway. I'm on a twelve on-stay-on shift. The Sheriff has a running gun battle with the Union over his new work schedules for us, half the force is ready to quit."

"Hey, Billy, cut us some slack. We'll all get together next week and do some fishing," Jack said.

Billy glanced at his watch and squinted up at the bright sky, "I don't know guys. The way these storms are rolling around, it might be a while before we can get too far out. I heard on the squawk-box coming over here that there is another big blow coming up this way from Cozumel. The outer rain bands are projected to hit us around 2300 tonight. You boys be real careful out there on the blue, don't wait too long to pull your hook and scoot for home if it gets too bad."

Once Billy was out of sight, Jack and Tommy pulled the two bags out of the dumpster and stuffed them into a fifty-five-gallon drum that had held motor oil for *The Girl's* two big motors. Tommy placed the locking band around the top cover and levered it down with a cheater-pipe, making it water and air tight. Satisfied with his handiwork, he then rolled the barrel to the back of the dive shop and placed it next to the wetsuit and diving gear drying racks where it was out of the way, but in plain sight.

The next two hours were spent moving the decompression chamber onto the aft deck of *The Girl*. Jack and Tommy were soaked in sweat from the effort of moving the cylinder to the dock, then winching it aboard the boat. Once centered fore-and-aft on the back deck, they dogged it down tight with chain and cables.

"This puppy ain't moving, I don't care what the weather throws at us," Tommy said.

Jack was wiping his face and neck with a sweat soaked towel thinking that putting the money on board *The Girl* was not necessarily the smartest place to put it, but at least he would know where it was. The best guess was that there was around seven million in the chamber, a couple million in the oil drum, and Ike had a million ... oh, and the bundles of cash in the walk-in reefer at the bar. Not a bad day's work, *if you can get it.* With Olsen out of the equation, the only others who knew he had the drug money were Don Cona and Ike. Jack didn't think Ike would get greedy and try anything, but the Don was a lethal threat that Jack wasn't sure how to deal with. Don Cona knew about the money and had implied that it was his in spite of Jack taking the risk. Twenty cents on the dollar would give him and Tommy a couple of million bucks, which wouldn't be that bad, considering it was free money. But why give up ten for two without a little push-back? The money in the chamber was safe for now. After tonight, if it looked like the Don was going to play nasty, then he would turn the money over to him and be happy with the two million cut.

The wild cards were still Gomez and the Sheriff. If Don Cona was right about Olsen being tied in with Gomez, and the Sheriff was, too, then was Gomez working one cop off the other? Did the Sheriff know about Jack, other than being Pointman's friend? The information from Billy Short was reassuring to Jack that the Sheriff probably did not know. Why else would he be pushing so hard to hunt down Point's killer? Also, the Sheriff had to know more about Gomez's missing ten million bucks than he was pretending to know, if only from the street rumors. Jack was sure the money was the real motive behind the big push on the special police squad to come up with information. Putting his thoughts together led Jack to the conclusion that the Sheriff was the primary threat. Any serious gunplay would come from that direction.

Chapter 9

It was evening. The tide flow was running faster than normal pushed by the storm forming out in the gulf, alerting skippers to double-check their anchor and mooring lines for the coming blow. The sky off to the southwest was an angry gray line sitting on the horizon, while a slight breeze was picking up, blowing another boiler of a day away, and bringing the tangy fishy-smell of ballyhoo and mangrove rot with it. Every living creature on the island gave a sigh of relief as the sun went down and night approached, having survived another day in paradise. Danger was also riding on the wind as *The Girl* rode her dock lines high and tight. Jack and Tommy had stripped off the canvas jumper that shaded the aft deck, and stowed it ashore in the dive hut, giving a clear deck for the expected load of *merchandise*. They didn't know how much space the cargo would take up, so they pulled off all unnecessary gear and equipment, trying to make *The Girl* as light as possible for added speed in case it was needed later that night. The decompression chamber took up half the deck space, but still allowed for easy movement along either side, plus storage of the unknown merchandise.

Tommy had topped off the main and reserve tanks with diesel and greased up every fitting and moving piece attached to the engine and gears. There was no room tonight for mechanical failure. Jack wanted this to be a quick get-in and get-out operation. Follow the orders of Cona's men, and hope that there would be no gunplay. This was the last place Jack wanted to be tonight, but Tony Cona had said that he should go along for the ride ... for the experience. Yeah right, like this was some big career move.

"Not scared are you, Jack?" Tommy asked, chewing a huge wad of double bubble, a sure sign that he was about to crap himself.

"Me, nah. As long as I have my pistol on me and know which way to swim when things go sour, I'll be just fine," he said, sounding more confident than he felt.

Jack knew if they just kept their heads and stayed alert for any double-cross or foul play, they would be ok. Jack had stripped and cleaned his pistol again, holstered it on a web belt that also carried his old Marine K-Bar knife and a can of pepper spray, and then stuffed it all into a canvas carry bag. Like they say, once you're in the Marines, you're never really out. You never forget the drilling or the combat training they beat into you, nor do you ever forget lessons on how to kill. On the taxi ride over to the dive shop, Jack was mentally busy trying to remember all the close-in hand-to-hand moves he had been taught. The only one really in focus was from his old Gunnery Sergeant, 'shoot first … and often, and if that doesn't stop the sumbitch, run.'

"Oh, before I forget, I put that .12-gauge street sweeper along with the box of flares in the small cabinet below the helm. I figured if we needed it quick that would be a good place for it," Tommy said.

"Let's just keep cool and be alert tonight. If we do like the Don said and follow Junior's directions, we'll make it back without any problems. On the other hand, let's keep our eyes and ears open for any sign of trouble for us. If it looks like we are going to get in a jam, let's just haul ass, shooting our way out if we have to. Let's go over the electronics and radio one more time just to be sure we're set," Jack said.

"I have both radios locked on channel 16 in case we run into some bad shit. All my waypoints from here to Havana are set on the GPS, and I have the Furama's ray dome on max sweep. If something goes wrong, one of us will need to get the signal out to the Coasties to send in the calvary," Tommy said.

"I figure we'll be in the water a couple of hours if we have to jump overboard before a boat arrives, and, with the gulf stream running at three to five knots, we could be off Big Pine by the time they find us," Jack said.

"Not to mention sharks," Tommy added seriously.

"Hey, as long as we have our K-bars, we'll wrestle those bad boys to the bottom."

"Spare me, Popeye."

While Tommy continued checking the electronics, Jack walked from stem to stern looking for anything out of place or something they may have overlooked that should go ashore. Out in the harbor, cooking smells were in the air from the anchored boats riding their anchor lines, bows pointing to the west on taut lines. The calm flat water of a couple of hours ago had turned into a chop with rougher water out beyond the break. Nautical twilight lay across the harbor... that time of day during which military men love to attack. It's not dark and it's not light, and shapes are difficult to define, objects appear to be what they aren't — Mother Nature's camouflage.

A medium-sized paneled truck rolled across the lot, crunching coral and shell gravel as it turned and backed in close beside the dive shop. The truck's brightly painted sides announced that it belonged to "Ted's Beds," a well-known provider of beds and mattresses at reasonable prices throughout the Keys. Jack and Tommy were immediately alert. They glanced at each other and walked over to the cab.

"What's up, Buddy? We weren't expecting any bed delivery," Tommy said.

"One of you Jack Marsh?" the man riding shotgun asked.

"That's me, but I didn't buy a bed."

"No sweat, we'll be going with you tonight. Is the boat ready?" the driver asked as he got out, sweeping his eyes across the lot and the harbor.

Jack felt a tinge of excitement as the passenger got out and made his own sweep. Whoever these guys were, they were definitely pros. Both men had on muscle tight T-shirts, jeans and jungle boots. Jack's first impression was Navy SEALs or Marine Recon. They had a no-nonsense air about them that oozed confidence and danger.

"Are there just the two of you?" Jack asked. "We were expecting more."

The driver slapped the side panel a couple of times as he walked to the back of the truck and rolled up the door. Four more copies of the first two guys jumped down, scanning the area with razor sharp eyes, taking in every detail in a flash.

"Is this our ride?" the driver asked pointing to *The Girl*.

"That's her. Welcome aboard. The only thing I ask is that if you use the head, don't pump it more than three times, or she'll back up on us," Tommy instructed.

Without a word, the six men pulled canvas cases out of the truck and loaded them below in the cabin. Once back on deck, the driver, whom Jack guessed to be the senior man, pointed at one of the men and then over to the Shrimp Bar a hundred yards away. The man quickly walked to the spot. The leader pointed to another man and designated the street side of the yard. *Guards out*, Jack thought, *these guys are definitely Special Ops of some kind.*

Once the leader was satisfied that his flanks were covered, he and the other three men pulled two large cases off the truck and placed them on the boat's deck. Jack had seen fiberglass cases like them before in Kuwait and had also seen what the contents could do to an Iraqi tank. Each case held a Flame Assault Shoulder Weapon, known in the trade as a FLAME. A round from one of those babies melted steel and evaporated flesh in less than a microsecond. The Army used them as a replacement for the old flame-throwers of Korea and Vietnam era. The FLAME held four rounds, each capable of major damage to a target. The tube frame could be reloaded, but generally it was discarded because it was too much of a burden to lug around empty in a combat situation.

"What are you guys expecting to go up against?" Jack asked the leader.

The man's only answer was a snapping of his fingers and the four men went below decks without another word. After about ten minutes, Jack stuck his head below and asked, "Is this it? We need instructions up here if you're expecting the boat to go anywhere anytime soon."

"Sit tight, we'll tell you when it's time," came the reply.

Tommy and Jack sat up by the bow waiting for whatever was supposed to happen next. Neither one of them could figure out what the Spec Ops guys were going to do with all that firepower in the cases. If their plan was to take out Castro, they couldn't have picked a better weapon system. The M202 was a mean mother, and unless Castro was inside some reinforced bunker, he could easily be vaporized in seconds. If he was in a car, on a lectern podium, or in a building, the man would definitely go down, and wouldn't be getting up without the help of a street scraper of some kind.

Jack had his eye on the weather front that was moving in as he watched the small dinghies in the harbor bobbing around like fishing corks, their painter lines taut to their mother ship's stern. The wind had picked up and was whistling through halyards and lines, sounding like the cries of sirens beckoning mariners to come closer. Gusts of wind carried a light rain, wetting down the coral dust and cooling the molten blacktops. In just a half hour, the temperature had dropped at least ten degrees, prompting Jack to pull a couple of rain slickers out of the bow locker for Tommy and himself.

"You think we ought to take a couple of slickers out to those guys on guard duty?" Tommy asked.

"Hell no, let 'em get wet. We're not in the Corps anymore, Tommy. Besides, I think they are swabbies anyway. Swabbies love being wet," Jack said with a smile.

"Looks like show time," Tommy said, nodding his head towards a dark sedan pulling in the lot.

The car sat in the dusk for a few minutes. Then, without any indication of a signal, the team leader came up from the cabin and walked out to the car. The back door opened and the man got in, closing the door behind him. Jack and Tommy sat looking on, feeling more and more like outsiders watching a mystery play out. After ten minutes, the leader got out on one side, another man from the other side, and then Junior. As soon as the doors closed, the sedan backed up and took off in the direction it had arrived.

The three men approached the boat without a word, jumped aboard, and went below decks. Tommy went back to the helm thinking that he would be given the order to launch at any minute, but fifteen minutes went by and … nothing. Still no marching orders.

"Hey, Junior, we have a storm front moving in so we'll need to get this party started pretty soon, or we won't make it out of the harbor," Tommy called out.

The hatch door opened and the new man stuck his shaved head out, "Shut the fuck up. We'll go when I say we go."

Ten minutes later, the bald guy and the team leader came out and went forward carrying a small piece of equipment that Jack recognized as an SSBT, a satellite short-burst transmitter. The two men huddled down over the unit for a few minutes, then closed it up, and went back down below.

"What the fuck," Tommy said, looking at Jack.

A minute later, Baldy came up, with Junior right behind him, "Gentlemen, let's roll."

"Uh, excuse me, but, roll to where?" Tommy asked, a little peeved at the man who came aboard *his* boat and started throwing out orders. "I need more than a 'Let's roll' from you if you expect to get anywhere tonight. Now let's do this right, give me the numbers where you want to go, your anticipated E.T.A., and the call signs of whoever it is we are meeting up with."

"I'll give you that data when I think you need it, now get us away from this dock and out of the harbor, Captain," Baldy said, giving a shrill whistle to the two sentries to get back aboard.

As Tommy argued with the bald guy, Jack had been watching Junior pace back and forth while talking on his cell phone. Whatever was being said, Junior did not look happy about it. Junior hung up with a snap of his wrist, shaking his head.

"What kind of trouble we have, Junior?" Jack asked.

Junior just shook his head and tried to walk around Jack. Jack stood his ground, "If I'm going to be putting my life on the line for the Don and this wild ass caper you guys have planned tonight, I want to know what the hell is happening. First off, who the hell is that Rambo guy back there and what's with the rocket launchers?"

"Jack, listen to me, the less you know the better off you'll be, but I'll tell you this much. The original plan has been trashed. We missed Gomez today in Miami and he's shooting every one of our guys he can find as payback. Don't ask me how he found out it was the Don that ordered the hit. He just knew. Besides that, he switched routes on us for tonight's cash drop. We picked up his bagman in Miami, and beat him until he told us about the switch. The man confessed that Gomez had to put up ten mil of his own money to cover last week's loss, then when we missed him today, he went to ground and changed the route."

"Sounds like it's just a turf war now. Things will calm down in a few weeks and will get back to normal," Jack offered.

"The Don is about to bust a gut over not getting his hands on tonight's wash money. I can tell you, Don Cona is not happy and has shooters sitting outside the Condor's

Biscayne compound, ready to blow the fucking place up. Thank God he has the ten million you're sitting on or else he would kill you, me, Tommy, and everybody who ever knew about it, touched it, smelled it, or heard about it if it turned up missing.

As Junior said this, Jack's heart skipped a beat knowing that Junior was just inches away from the hidden money. Suddenly, this became the moment of truth. Jack knew he would not be able to keep the money and live. He was in way over his head to even think he could outmaneuver the Mafia and the cartel, much less the Sheriff and his special team. Just seeing the Special Operations people on board *The Girl* was warning enough that he was up against something so big he couldn't even identify who it was exactly he was up against. He made his decision.

"Junior, tonight when we get back, I want you to take this to the Don," Jack said as he tapped the decompression chamber.

Junior looked confused. He looked at Jack, then at the chamber, and back to Jack.

"What?"

"*This*," Jack said tapping the chamber again.

"This *what*?" Junior said, totally perplexed.

"*The fucking money, Junior*. It's in here … Jeezus, man."

Junior looked at the chamber thoughtfully, then broke into a huge smile. "You telling me there's ten million dollars inside this thing?" Junior said in awe.

"I'm telling you that the Don's money is inside here ..." Jack started to say how much, but the bald guy came up unannounced.

"Once we're out on open water, we'll have a meeting on deck with everyone," he said and strode off using the chamber to help balance himself.

"Well, fuck me, Jack. You are one clever Mick. Nobody would ever think to look there. Holy crap, is the Don ever going to get a laugh out of this," Junior said wrapping his arms around Jack, pulling him into a huge bear hug.

Tommy pulled away from the dock, passed slowly by the loud music and laughter from the Shrimp Bar, slipped through the channel's no-wake zone out of the harbor, then went a mile out to the rock pile marker. Tommy checked his position, scanned the horizon for any hazards or other craft, saw that all was clear, and threw the wheel over onto a 180° heading, due south, straight for Cuba. With two-thirds throttle, The Girl quickly came up on plane and skimmed across the water. The big motors roared with power, sending a comforting vibration up through the hull.

Rain slanting in from a strong southwest wind was shearing across the starboard bow soaking the decks and drenching the men in the cockpit. Tommy was busy watching for anything floating in *The Girl's* path and also keeping an eye on the radar and GPS. Five miles out on the 180° course, the head man of the team signaled Tommy to power down.

Jack did a double-take when all the men came up from the cabin dressed in black from head to foot. Exposed skin and faces were painted a flat black, web gear and harnesses were also black.

"For those who don't know me, my name is Colonel Carson, Delta Command. You will be taking orders from me over the next few days. I am to be obeyed without question during the infiltration phase, the execution phase, and exfiltration. Each of you knows exactly what you are expected to do," the Colonel said, hands on hips. "First Sergeant Otis is your team leader. He will ensure that my orders are carried out promptly and completely. Any sandbagging and you answer to me," the Colonel paused again for effect. "The highest command authority is watching this action personally. I will not disappoint him, gentlemen. We will succeed in our mission even if we all have to die to achieve it ... *OooRah!"* The Colonel yelled.

The silence was deafening. Not a peep out of the six professionals. These men had been together for several years in some of the meanest spots on earth...they were experienced in death and killing. To be talked to like this was an insult to their professionalism.

"Colonel, the men know what to do and they'll carry out their mission. They won't disappoint you, *Sir*," First Sergeant Otis said.

All the team members let out a loud *"OooRah!"* then ducked back down the hatch out of the rain. Colonel Carson was left standing red-faced … actually pea-green faced from the LED lighting from the electronics console.

"Fucking wise-ass," the Colonel mumbled to himself, then turned to Tommy. "There's been a change in plans, Capitán. The original plan was for us to hook up with General Santos out here in the Straits and transfer over to his craft." The Colonel paused, giving Junior a condescending look. "But our Mafia allies screwed the pooch and got greedy trying to kill the Cartel's Miami man over ten million bucks in drug money. It seems like El Condor got a little upset about being on the receiving end of a block of C4 this afternoon and contacted his Cuban and Mexican connections, throwing a monkey wrench into our plans. General Santos has gone missing and Señor Castro, ever the sly one, is on alert for trouble. The perfect cover to slip my team into Cuba was blown by these clowns. A simple drug transaction in the Florida Straits and it gets fucked up by amateurs," the Colonel said, looking at Junior.

"Be careful, Colonel. I am not one of your men who you can talk that way to," Junior said with a murderous look.

"Never mind, Junior. You're too low on the shit list to matter. You're along because I was ordered to bring you along. Seems the boys in D.C. don't want to sever ties completely with you thugs. Fucking politicians."

"So what's the plan, are we still meeting someone out here? Where am I supposed to take us?" Tommy asked.

The Colonel handed Tommy a slip of paper with a GPS number on it. "Punch this in. I need the estimated time and distance to that location, not one meter left or right of it, Skipper."

Tommy got busy punching in the latitude and longitude numbers on the GPS as Jack checked the radar for any surface shipping. The rain was slanting down in sheets with wind gusts up to thirty knots. The seas were running high, causing the *Girl's* bow to pitch up and slam down as she cut through the waves.

"Are you nuts?" Tommy said looking up from the GPS screen. "That's almost fucking Havana. We're not going to Havana, Colonel. If you want to go fine, but not on this boat," Tommy declared.

"That's not Havana, and don't tell me where we are going. We're going to that spot. Those are the orders given to me, and now I'm giving them to you," Colonel Carson snarled.

"Wait a minute, cowboy, I'm not one of your men who you can order around like that. I'm the Skipper of this boat and …"

The Colonel snapped a pistol out of his waist band and fired, hitting Tommy in the shoulder, and knocking him down. Jack grabbed the Colonel's arm and pushed it up in the air as another round went off. Both men tumbled to the deck fighting for control of the pistol. Carson punched Jack in the nose and pulled his hand free, placing the muzzle between Jack's eyes.

"Back off or you're dead," Carson said, pulling the hammer back.

Jack rolled backwards holding his bleeding nose and crawled over to Tommy. Blood covered the front of Tommy's slicker and mixed with rainwater on the deck.

"You asshole! You shot Tommy. You're fucking insane, man!" Jack yelled over the howling wind. "Junior, grab the helm and hold us on course. Give it a little throttle so we stop rolling."

As Junior went to the helm, Carson kept the pistol trained on both men.

"I am in charge here. We're going to those coordinates and we're going now," Carson commanded. "Marsh, take the helm. Junior, pull Hicks down below and have the medic take a look at him. We're running behind schedule, gentlemen."

Jack was still breathing hard from the struggle with Carson as he kept the bow pointed into the waves with one hand and used a rag to stop his nosebleed with the other. The nose didn't feel broken, but it was swelling up, causing his eyes to squint. Jack spit a mouthful of blood out and watched as it mixed with the salt water sloshing around on the deck and quickly washed into the scuppers and over the side.

"Have you got the course plotted, Marsh?"

"No. I want to know what your game plan is before we go any further. You plan on killing us when we get you where you want to go?" Jack asked.

"Why would I want to kill you? You get me to my destination, then you and your numbskull buddy can go anywhere you want. But, I'll tell you this. I will kill you if you don't do as I say and get me there pronto," Carson said as he pointed the pistol at Jack's head again.

The two men stared at each other for a few moments as the rain poured down and the boat rode the mounting waves.

"You win, Colonel. mainly because I don't have a choice. But I don't trust you and I'll be glad to be done with you. I'll get you there, and then you can get the fuck off this boat."

Junior popped his head up from below, "Looks like a straight through shot. Went in the shoulder and came out below the shoulder blade. The medic says no problem.

Tommy will be sore, but fine. He's got the bleeding stopped and the wounds stitched closed," Junior said smiling.

"That's good news, Junior Thanks," Jack said, then continued plotting the course.

"Colonel, I have our course set. It's not a straight-in as you wanted, but it gets us there alive and faster, actually. I have us hitting Sand Key first, then moving on a 165° line to Caya Piscada, then down a 180° line to Santa Cruz del Norte. Santa Cruz is a small village west of Havana. That's your destination based on the numbers you gave Tommy. He was right. It's damned close to Havana, so any mistakes and we'll be inside one of El Presidenté's prison for a few years."

"Let's move it, Skipper, clock's ticking."

Jack swung over to his new course and throttled up. The bow slammed into the waves, soaking the prow and cockpit. Anything that had been dry was now soaked. The wind was wild, coming in from every direction with stinging rain. The only light came from the electronic console. Jack had flipped all the running lights off once he had his course set. The radar reached out twelve miles, looking for any navigational threats or other shipping traffic. The depth under the keel was thirty fathoms, engine rpm's were turning a smooth 2300, oil was pumping through the engine's arteries keeping them cool, along with the saltwater intakes. Everything was working as it should.

Through the wind gusts and water washing aboard, the radio crackled — "Motor Vessel *Island Girl*, MV *Island Girl*, this is U.S. Coast Guard Vessel Mobile, come in," the radio squawked.

Jack's eyes grew large as he picked up the hand mike, "Mobile, this is *Island Girl*." Jack answered, as the Colonel raised his pistol to Jack's head signaling him with a finger to his lips. Jack shook his head in acknowledgement.

"*Island Girl*, switch over to channel thirty-two."

Jack dialed in channel 32 and acknowledged back to the Mobile.

"*Island Girl*, we show you on a course that will take you out of territorial waters if you proceed on a 180° track. State your intentions, over."

"Mobile, *Island Girl*. My plan is to run laps south of Sand Key to check out new stabilizers in this storm, R.T.B., return to base tomorrow afternoon, over."

"Roger, *Island Girl*. Be advised that current forecast projects this weather to hit a Cat 1 by 24:00 tonight, with a small craft warning in effect until 16:00 tomorrow. We recommend that you return to port immediately."

"Roger, Mobile, return to port recommended. I'll try to finish up testing by 24:00 and RTB at that time," Jack said.

"Roger, *Island Girl*. Also be advised of unusual Cuban Naval activity south of Sand Key, east to Caya Piscada, and west to Playa Norte. Intentions unknown. Report any sightings, please. U.S. Coast Guard Vessel Mobile out."

"Good, real good, Marsh," Carson said patting Jack on the shoulder.

Chapter 10

Jack didn't like the news about the Cuban Navy being in the area as it increased the risk considerably. Even though most Cuban vessels had old or unreliable electronic equipment, they were very well-armed with the latest surface to surface missiles. Furnished by North Korea and Venezuela, as brotherly gestures, they failed to be trained in using them correctly. But the Cubans have a great eye, and line of sight is clear out on open water. Jack was confident that the storm would help hide him from any nosey water patrol craft that came within a twelve-mile range of his radar scan. If nothing else, he could turn away from the oncoming ship and just outrun it. His main concern, besides the storm, was his return trip. The run into Santa Cruz would take five hours, if the storm didn't shift to the south, causing him to run against a strong headwind. If that happened, it could add another couple of hours to the trip. Figure a half hour to drop the team off and then scoot north for home. It would be tight to get in, get out, and get away before the sun came up. Bad equipment or not, the Cubans could spot him easily in the daylight. Then it would be a decision to surrender or try and outrun them.

The next two hours were monotonous, but dangerous, as the storm's intensity grew. Waves were roaring over the bow continuously, giant explosions of lightning flashed overhead as the rain grew heavier. The *Island Girl* was holding her own against the raging storm and answering the helm with each twist and turn. Jack was getting tired from the constant strain of holding the course. If the GPS was correct, Sand Key was off a half mile to starboard and he would make his course correction in the next couple of minutes to Caya Piscada. Once past Sand Key, the bottom dropped to several hundred feet until they drew closer to the Caya Piscada, which was nothing more than a coral rock pile sticking out of the water that the Arawak Indians had used as a fishing layover back before Columbus.

The hatch door slid open, and the Colonel, with one of the team members, came out on deck and they made their way to the back fantail. They quickly set up a satellite radio, and the two huddled over the small piece of equipment for a few minutes, then broke it down and hurried back to the cockpit out of the rain.

"Anything new from your people?" Jack asked, as the two passed by him.

The Colonel just looked at Jack, then down to his watch, "You need to crank this bucket up and get us there. It seems Fidel is sending out the fleet to stop any *Yanqui* aggressors who might try to invade his worker's paradise tonight. I don't want to be caught out here in the open water, so shake the kinks out of those motors, and let's go."

Jack decided to bypass Caya Piscada and go directly into Santa Cruz. This would cut some time off the clock, and hopefully avoid any patrol boats sitting in the lee of the island riding out the storm while waiting for the *Yanquis* to show up. He inputted the new data into the GPS and it flashed the new course, time and distance within a second. Jack adjusted the wheel for a 173° course that would take them right into the little cove that Santa Cruz sat in. Once he was closer, he would go right a few degrees to land the men to the west of the village.

Junior came up from below with a mug of coffee and handed it to Jack.

"I heard the Colonel tell the men that, in spite of the storm and the screw up with the original plan, the assault on Castro is still on," Junior said.

Jack took a quick look at Junior, "I've got a bad feeling about the Colonel, Junior. I think the plan is to leave no witnesses behind when they go ashore. I guess my question to you is whose side are you on? Are you just along for the ride, or are you part of the team down there?"

"Jack, my job was to make sure that the Colonel and his men got aboard the *Island Girl* okay, and then to see that they got off okay. After that, the Don said they are on their own."

"So, that means if Carson decides to pop us as he fades into the jungle, then you're one of the targets, right? In that case, we better be talking about some kind of plan to get away, don't you think?"

"Yeah, I'm not worried about those Special Ops guys down there, but the Colonel is nuts. I heard a couple of the guys saying that Carson's actually CIA, and that he had been on another Op with them in Bosnia a few years back. The Colonel went wild in a small village and shot the place up."

"Swell, a war crimes maggot in charge," Jack smirked.

"Yeah, even the Don don't go for that. You don't shoot women and kids, unless they earned it. Then it's ok."

Jack took a quick look at Junior to see if he was joking or not. The expression on the Mafia bodyguard's face didn't change. He believed what he had just said.

"When we get closer in, I'll get Tommy up here to sit at the helm. You take the bow, and I'll take the stern. Anything looks out of line, we shoot the Colonel. If the Ops guys want a piece of the action, I guess we'll have a regular firefight on deck," Jack said.

Twenty-five miles off Santa Cruz, Jack throttled back to idle, letting the boat wallow in the heavy seas. Two blinking dots had suddenly appeared on the radar screen about five miles off the port bow, moving in an east–west course. Jack was surprised that the radar hadn't picked up the two vessels sooner, like twelve miles further out. He checked the radar for any problems but couldn't find any, so chalked it up to the storm.

Carson burst out of the hatch, "What's wrong? I didn't tell you to stop. Get this piece of shit moving, mister," he shouted over the storm noise.

Jack tapped the radar, pointing out the two blips. "We have company nearby. We need to sit tight for a few minutes to see what they're up to," he said.

The *Island Girl* was bouncing in five directions at the same time as water poured over the sides. The rain hammered down so it seemed as if it were a wall of water. Jack could hear someone vomiting below deck and knew they would have company topside very soon. He knew from experience that sea sickness in a confined space was highly contagious. Once one man started puking, everyone puked. Junior suddenly grabbed his throat and threw up all over the deck, with Carson a split second behind him. Jack breathed shallowly through his mouth, concentrating on the oncoming vessels. The rain and salt water on the deck washed the puke into the scuppers, but the smell was still heavy in the air.

"Get this boat moving, that's an order, mister!" Carson yelled over the howling wind.

At that second, a terrific flash and explosion hit the *Island Girl*. The smell of ozone was so heavy it gagged the men on deck. The two engines shut down — the boat was dead in the water.

"What the fuck was that? The bastards are shooting at us," the Colonel screamed and ducked below the console frame, hiding his head in his arms.

Jack stepped out of the cockpit and saw that the radar dome was gone. Lightning had made a direct hit on it and vaporized it. Back at the controls, he cranked up the engines with no problem, and then a few seconds later, the port engine quit and wouldn't start back up. Most of the electronics powered back up, except for the bilge pump and the cabin lights.

"How's it look, Marsh?" Carson asked as he stood up from his position of relative safety behind the hatch door.

Jack ignored him and continued his inspection. "Junior, grab the helm. I'm going down to check on the port motor."

Jack grabbed a flashlight, ducked inside the cabin, and then stepped down into the motor area. The prop shaft on the starboard engine was turning and running true, gas filter looked good, and the oil pressure was good. He turned his attention to the port engine and saw immediately what the problem was. The fuel pump was clogged with seaweed and sand. It would have to be taken off and cleaned, which under the present situation wasn't practical.

Back up topside, Jack delivered the news. "Lightning took out the radar, and the port engine is down. Otherwise we're okay. We can still make it to Santa Cruz, but it will take us at least a couple of hours, which would put us in there at around 03:00. Good for the Ops guys, but bad for us on the boat trying to get away in daylight. Another problem is that we are blind. Without the radar, we don't know who is coming our way until we see them. Before we lost the radar, there were two vessels out to our ten o'clock position moving left to right across our bow. That was fifteen minutes ago. If we have been spotted, we can expect to either to be shot at or captured, so keep your eyes open," Jack reported.

Junior and Carson stood, continuing to look at Jack as if waiting for instructions.

"Colonel, get a couple of men up forward, and two aft as lookouts. Any sign of the Cubans and we'll try to outrun them, maybe disappear in this storm," Jack ordered. "Junior, stay with Tommy below. Make sure that he can take over the helm if need be, and bring him up to speed on our situation," Jack said with a discreet wink.

A few minutes later, Jack watched as the Colonel and the First Sergeant cracked open one of the cases of M202s and placed it under the cockpit overhead to keep out of the rain.

"If those commie bastards come within a quarter mile of us, I'm lighting them up," Carson said with an evil grin.

Jack noticed the First Sergeant roll his eyes and look away. This gave Jack hope that, if the shit hit the fan, the Spec Op boys would back him up … maybe.

The *Island Girl* continued to wallow, up and down, side to side. Everyone on deck was soaked and chilled to the bone. Jack thought he saw a running light and a green starboard light directly to their front through the torrents of rain, but then quickly lost sight of it in the darkness. He decided to wait another fifteen minutes, then make for Cuba.

An hour and a half later, Jack throttled back, barely keeping forward momentum. The land mass ahead was discernable only as a blacker black than the rest of the night. An occasional explosion of lightning did little to tell him what was ahead. He was relying on the GPS for his depth, but for any submerged obstacles or coral heads, he was on his own. Tommy was sitting on the deck at Jack's feet with the street sweeper shotgun in his hands, semi-alert for any treachery. The two bow guards were instructed to watch for any submerged objects and to sing out if they spotted anything. It was a useless order since the water was blacker than the land.

As the *Island Girl* slipped inside the small cove, the wind died off. Blocked by the land to starboard, the water was still turbulent but nothing like the wild ride outside on the open water. Jack could see a line of gray ahead that he recognized as a sand beach and kept his course straight in. As he approached the beach, he saw that the shoreline hooked around to his starboard side, creating another, smaller hidden cove. He swung the helm over and ran parallel to the beach, aiming for the calm waters. The beach arced around into the cove and Jack throttled back, creeping forward, watching his depth as he went, fifteen feet ... twelve ... eight ... he felt the bow keel nudge into the sand. They had arrived.

The next few minutes were a blur of activity as Jack and a couple of the Ops men set a stern anchor out and tied off two lines on stout coconut trees on the beach. The *Island Girl* wasn't going anywhere without those trees dragging along with her. Once the boat was secure, the Ops guys offloaded their personal equipment, placing it inside the tree line, off the beach, then came back for the M202 cases. The rockets were manhandled over the side and through the shallow water, then placed with the other gear.

Colonel Carson came out of the cabin dressed in black head to foot like the other men. "Junior, come on over here. I need to talk to you men before I go ashore," Carson ordered.

"Nah, I'm okay back here. I need to watch for sharks," Junior said holding up his pistol for Carson to see.

Without hesitation, Carson raised his pistol and popped off a round, knocking Junior over the transom and into the water. Jack flinched from the suddenness of the action, and, when he looked again, the pistol was pointed at his head.

"Hey! I thought we were free to go," Jack yelled. "What the fuck did you shoot Junior for?"

"You didn't think that we could let you go back did you? You know too much. You and that shitbird in the water could tell the world about what happened out here. No, Chump, this show is mine. You're not getting any of the glory. Castro is my ticket, nobody else's," Colonel Carson said as he placed the barrel between Jack's eyes. "Thanks for the ride."

Carson's head exploded in a spray of blood and bone, hitting Jack's face and chest. Carson's lifeless body dropped to the deck with a thump. Jack wiped the gore off his face and out of his eyes, then threw up. Tommy pulled himself up from the corner he had been sitting in and also upchucked.

"You okay, Marsh?" the First Sergeant asked as he came back aboard. "I knew that bastard was going to try something like this, piece of shit," he said, giving the body a kick.

"Yeah, I'm okay, but we need to help Junior."

"Two men are already in the water pulling him out." The team leader turned and gave a whistle. Two more of the team jumped aboard.

"Pull this asshole ashore and bury him inside the tree line. Don't waste a lot of time, we're out of here in two minutes," he said, checking his watch. "It's going to be daylight in another hour, I would suggest you hole up here for the day and make it back tonight. Just make sure you're far away from Cuba by this time tomorrow. The Indians are going to have their war paint on and will be looking for white scalps."

"Yeah, First Sergeant. We'll be gone."

Two of the Ops men laid Junior on the deck as a third wrapped a bandage around his bloody waist.

"Stomach shot, keep him from bleeding out if you can," the medic said, then was back over the side wading to the beach.

The First Sergeant gave a twirling hand signal over his head, "Charlie-Mike, boys, *continue mission.*"

—

Jack and Tommy watched the team slip silently into the tree line and disappear. Both men were tired and wet as they surveyed their surroundings. The cove was actually a very beautiful secluded spot with a white sand beach and a coconut grove that went back into the land a few hundred feet, then turned into a giant hardwood forest. It didn't appear that anyone lived on the beach or had been there for a while because of the trash strewn about from the tides. Jack went to Junior and pulled him over to the hatch, then gently down the two steps into the cabin. The cabin smelled of vomit, sweat, and blood. Jack made Junior comfortable on one of the bunks, then checked the stomach wound. The bullet had made a perfectly round hole to the left of his bellybutton. It was puckered and burned black around the edges with watery blood oozing out. Jack took a roll of gauze from the first aid kit that was kept aboard and sprinkled a glob of sulfa powder into the wound, then plugged the hole up with a wad of gauze. Jack looked up and saw Junior staring at him.

"Is this it, Jacky? Do I need to say my prayers?" Junior asked.

"Are you kidding? You'll be up good as new as soon as I get you home. Just sleep and I'll watch over you."

"Thanks, Jacky. I won't forget this," Junior said and closed his eyes.

On deck, Tommy was sitting at the helm trying to pick up the NOAA weather report, but there was so much static it was too garbled to understand clearly. Lightning was still popping across the sky and hadn't let up at all. The storm had to be at least a Cat 1 hurricane by now. The wind was tearing across the tops of the hills around the cove. They were anchored in a little fishhook-shaped cove with the *Island Girl* anchored on the hook end of the shape, totally out of the turbulent waters outside the bay.

"Tommy, you stay topside and watch for visitors. Anyone drops by, bang on the deck. I'm going down to clean out the fuel pump so we'll have both motors running when it's time to scoot."

"I'm not going anyplace, not with this chest ready to kill me."

"Oh, stop with the drama. Didn't you hear the corpsman? He said you were in great shape, million dollar wound, going home tonight ... ooh rah, Marine!" Jack said, smiling at his friend before ducking through the hatch.

When Jack came back up topside, the sky was still as dark as it had been two hours earlier. He checked his watch and saw it was 10:00 A.M. Tommy was asleep with his head on his arms, leaning on the GPS. Jack helped him down below and laid him out across from Junior. The food locker held a good assortment of canned foods, mostly soups and fruit. Jack poured four cans of vegetable soup into a pot, fired up the alcohol stove, and sat while it heated up.

"That smells good," Junior said groggily and tried to sit up, then fell back in pain.

"Junior, I'm not sure if you should eat or not with that stomach wound," Jack said.

"Gimme some, I'll let you know," Junior said as he pulled a cup of the hot soup to his lips.

Jack woke up Tommy and gave him a cup, then poured himself a cup. The beating of the rain and the hot soup made Jack sleepy. He hadn't had more than four hours of sleep since all this started. When they got back, he was going to sleep for a week. Maybe check into a hotel, somewhere he wouldn't be bothered, and just ... sleep.

Chapter 11

Jack snapped his head up. Something had awakened him. He checked his watch, 2:30 p.m. Crap, he had been asleep for almost three hours. Tommy and Junior were sleeping soundly. Jack heard the noise again. It sounded like someone was hitting the hull with a stick. Jack pulled his pistol out of his waistband and stuck his head out the hatch.

A short man with denim jeans and a T-shirt was standing on the shore in the downpour, ready to throw another rock when he spotted Jack.

"Señor, are you Ok?" the man yelled in heavily accented English.

"Yeah, I'm fine. I anchored in here until the storm moves on, then I will leave. Is that OK?" Jack said as he stepped up to the railing.

"Sure, why not?" the man shrugged. "It is a free country, Señor." The man cackled at his own joke.

"Maybe I go with you when you leave? My brother lives in Miami. What do you say?" The man asked.

"Not this trip, my friend. I am only going as far as Key West," Jack said.

"But, Señor, I think you are going to need an interpreter when you leave the safety of this small bay. The State Policía is busy looking for Norte Americano criminals at this very minute, just over there." The man pointed to the hills and the Strait beyond. "I myself watched them, not one hour ago."

"What is your name?" Jack asked.

"My name is Michael. It means closest to God, Señor. I am blessed with good luck all my life. It was God's angel, Michael, who led me to this very spot today. He says this is my lucky day. A gringo is coming to get me in a big boat and take me to Miami," the man smiled.

"Michael, do you know anything about working on a boat ... how to work on deck?" Jack asked, thinking that an extra pair of hands might be helpful if he had to try and outrun the Cuban Navy.

"Señor, I was born on a boat. Of course I know how to work the ropes and things. I am also a very good cook and I am honest. Sure, give Michael a try. You will be surprised at what he can do."

"Come on aboard, then," Jack yelled over the storm's noise overhead.

Michael raised a finger, signaling one moment and ran into the grove. A minute later, he ran back out pulling a small boy by his hand and a suitcase in the other.

"Hold on," Jack yelled. "Who is that?"

"This small child, Señor? This is my son, Michael Ortega Junior. He always goes where I go. It is our custom in

Cuba, Señor," Michael Senior answered and hurried aboard the boat.

Jack stood watching the tree line for a few minutes, sensing danger around him. He had screwed up by dozing off like that. It was a careless act that could have gotten all their throats cut. Even though the storm hadn't let up, Jack wanted to get out on the water and make a run for it. Given the chance, he felt that the *Island Girl* could outrun most of the smaller coastal craft that the Cubans used.

Jack went below to let everyone know that they were pulling out. "Tommy, I want you to stay below here with Junior and little Mike here. Stay in the bunks and hold on, we're going to be bouncing and slamming hard out there," Jack said.

"And me, Señor?" Michael asked, anxious to be of help.

"You'll be topside with me. I want everyone to put on life vests now. Once we're out there, if anything happens we won't have time to be looking for jackets."

Jack noticed that little Mike was spooning out the last of the soup from the pan, wide-eyed and gobbling it down. He opened a small storage cupboard, pulled out a handful of packaged beef jerky and sausages, and gave them to Mike.

"Do you speak English, Miguel?" Jack asked.

"Yes sir, my father is a fine teacher at the University and he insists that I speak only English at home. My sister,

Consuela, she speaks better English than I do, but she is no longer with us," he said, his voice dropping.

"Miguel, shhh!" Michael Senior said sharply. "Forgive him, Señor; he has a fever from the storm."

"Come on, Big Mike, we have work to do," Jack said, stepping up to the deck.

Jack cranked up the port motor first and let it warm up, and then he hit the starboard motor. The batteries turned the engine over, but it failed to start. Jack was sure he had removed all the debris from the pump and filter. He hit the starter again and held it. The powerful batteries turned the motor, the motor belched, spit, spluttered, and then roared into life. Jack felt a wave of relief flood over him. Now he had a chance to make good their escape.

Big Mike jumped over the side and untied one line from the coconut palm, then the other line. Back on deck, he coiled the lines expertly and went to the back transom, ready to pull up the stern anchor once Jack signaled to do so.

Jack had reset the GPS for 00°, due north. Key West was off on a 355° bearing, but Jack's plan was to clear the cove, haul ass straight up into the Gulf Stream, and then adjust coordinates once they were clear of Cuban waters. If their luck held, they would be clear of Cuban waters in about two hours and back in Key West in another four or five, at a speed of twelve to thirteen knots an hour.

Jack pulled the engines into reverse, turning only a few rpm's, and listened to the motors churn up the water aft. The boat didn't move. Jack gave the engines more gas, and the water off the transom boiled as the props tried to pull the hull out of the sand. Jack saw the problem and reversed the port engine to forward and then gave the starboard more gas, forcing the keel off to an angle in the sand. Jack quickly reversed the engines to go the other way … and *Island Girl* slipped free of the sand. Jack spun the helm as the boat backed out, and then he moved the control handles forward, spun the helm the other way, and stopped once the bow was pointed out to sea. He took a deep breath, checked his GPS bearing, and opened the throttles up, making the *Girl* jump forward and up on plane before she cleared the cove. Big Mike had a huge grin on his face as he held on to the windscreen brace.

"Hahaha," he laughed, looking back at the receding strip of beach. "I am free. I am free. Fuck you, Fidel," he yelled into the wind.

"Don't celebrate yet. We're not out of trouble for a couple of hours," Jack yelled over all the noise from the motors roaring and the storm raging around them.

Jack had a quick flash of sitting in his car as it went through an automatic car wash and the feeling of claustrophobia it had given him. The *Island Girl* was clearing the cove and running straight into a hundred car washes, each gone mad. The boat hit the storm wall and bucked up into the air as if hit on the chin with a sledge hammer. Then it was a wild bronco ride, fighting to keep forward movement while being slugged from the right and left, with an occasional rabbit punch to the stern. What was left of the radar pylon tore free and slammed into the windscreen, knocking the whole port tempered-glass window out. Wind howled through the cockpit like crazed banshees looking for souls to drown.

Jack snapped his life vest buckle onto the helm and tightened it down so his stomach and chest were tight against the wheel. His knuckles were blue from the death grip he had on the helm. One of the bow lines that had been used to tie off to the coconut trees was cracking in the air like a hundred-foot whip in the hands of some unknown monster. The other line was still tied to the port bow up front, but its length was submerged over the side, sure to get tangled in one of the props. Jack's eyes burned from the saltwater peppering his face. He turned to tell Big Mike to get below, but saw that he was gone. Jack was shocked. A moment ago Mike was by his side holding on, and wiping the saltwater out of his eyes, and now he was gone. Jack throttled back, thinking that he would be able to spot the bright orange life vest in the surf. Once the forward speed was cut, the bow sunk down and the *Island Girl* began to pitch and corkscrew crazily.

Jack wiped his eyes and peered into the water as far out as his vision could see. A flash of orange was over off the port side, then it was gone. Jack saw the bow line go taut and realized that Mike had somehow grabbed it when he hit the water and was hanging on. Hesitantly, Jack unsnapped his life vest from the helm and crawled forward to where the line hung off the side and began to pull. He didn't dare stand up for fear of being knocked or blown over the side, and then they would all be lost. He pulled without looking over the side and suddenly became violently sick, throwing up on his slicker. After an eternity, the line was all in with Mike tied to it. Jack pulled the unconscious form onto the deck using all of his strength. Kneeling over the waterlogged body, Jack pushed hard on the little man's diaphragm with all his might, then three more quick pumps. He stuck his finger in Mike's mouth and pulled out a long piece of ingested seaweed. Mike coughed violently, gasped, then coughed again, spitting out slimy water then sucked in air to fill his lungs. Jack sat back and watched for a couple of minutes, catching his breath.

Crawling, Jack pulled Michael back to the cockpit, then down into the cabin. The smell of vomit hit both men and made them gag. Little Mike was rolled up in a ball on the deck crying and puking. Tommy was on the bunk with arms and legs locked against the bulkhead so he wouldn't roll out. His face was covered in smeared vomit and snot. The bandage covering his wound was bloody and wet. Junior was unconscious, or perhaps dead, but Jack couldn't be completely sure just by looking.

"Stay down below and help these guys," Jack yelled to Mike and then went topside into the storm.

The engines responded immediately when Jack hit the throttles and turned the bow back on course. The *Island Girl* jumped into the storm with a vengeance, as if she had a mind of her own. Once they had forward movement, Jack's seasickness slacked off and he was able to concentrate on keeping them alive. He checked his watch — 3:30 — another half hour and they should be out of Cuban waters. The storm was unbelievable. It should have blown through the area by now, but evidently it was stalled or hooking back. Whatever the reason, Jack was just thankful that the boat was still seaworthy and afloat. He was worried about Junior's stomach wound and thought back to his Marine training and different types of gunshot wounds. The most vivid in his memory was the sucking chest wound, where air filled the chest cavity, putting pressure on the heart and lungs, and causing death. A gut or stomach shot was survivable, but prone to massive infection and rapid toxic shock if not treated quickly. But under the current circumstances, there was nothing he could do but try and get him back home and into a hospital. Big and Little Mike were another problem. What the hell was he going to do with two Cuban illegals? What the hell had he been thinking when he told the older Mike to come aboard, and what the hell was he doing out here?

Jack twisted his head around to see how the chamber was riding under all the tossing and turmoil. The dogging securing the decompression chamber appeared to be holding. He smiled at the thought that there was seven million dollars right behind him, riding out one of the worst storms to hit the Florida Straits in years. Jack didn't know if that was true or not about the storm, but from his perspective it was the worst storm … ever. Jack laughed at his summation of his predicament. He swore to himself that if he survived this little venture, he was never leaving the Sand Bar sober again.

A piece of the transom flew up into the air and was carried away by the wind. Jack watched it, puzzled as it disappeared. Suddenly, another piece disintegrated, and then another, then a loud ricochet zinged off the chamber. Realization hit him like a bunker buster … they were under fire! Jack's head swung off to the left as another three holes punched into the deck. Out a hundred yards was a patrol boat bearing down on them with a flashing light coming from the bow. It took less than a second to know the flashing light was a machine gun shooting at them. Jack swung the helm to port trying to make his profile smaller, at the same time he firewalled the throttles. The *Girl* responded with a powerful thrust and tried to fly out of the water. Jack looked back and saw the patrol vessel had lost ground when it tried to match Jack's turn. The *Girl* was eating her way through the mountains of water that poured under the keel. As she mounted a huge wave, her props cleared the water and sent violent vibrations through the hull, then fell back, biting into the sea. For the moment, the patrol craft was lost in the storm behind a wall of rain and waves.

Jack kept the throttles at maximum thrust as he looked back over his shoulder for the Cubans to reappear. He took a deep breath and just as he thought he had lost them, a huge flash enveloped him. Tiny darts of pain stung his body as a fireball bellowed up and whipped away in the wind. Behind him, one of the chamber's tie-downs had broken loose but was still holding firm. The back transom was hanging off into the water, and the fiberglass deck was peeled back a few feet. If Jack throttled back, seawater would flow into the boat and down into the engine room compartment. Jack spun the helm to starboard and headed into a dense wall of rain while he watched to see if there was any fire coming from aft. The chamber broke free from the forward tie-downs and swung at an angle as Jack made the turn, causing it to slam into the port gunnel, knocking a five-foot section open to the ocean. The engines were still responding with power to the props, but the helm was feeling sluggish. Maybe a few rounds had hit the hull below the water line, allowing sea water to pour in.

Jack kicked the hatch door open, stuck his head in and yelled, "We may be going for a swim soon. Everybody up, put on extra life jackets. Put them around your chest, back, and waist. When we go in, we want to be bobbing like corks."

As Jack straightened up, the bow and pulpit disappeared in a ball of flame and fire that shook the hull from stem to stern. Water began pouring into the boat each time the *Girl* dropped into a trough and fought her way up the next mountain of water. Jack knew it was just a matter of minutes before the boat was swamped and sank, but he still fought the helm, trying to keep her on course. He wanted to get as much distance as he could between him and the Cuban craft before they had to abandon ship. The boat radio antenna was gone, lost somewhere back by the cove when the wind took all the aerial whips and antennas off. Jack still sent a May-Day out, knowing there was little, if any, chance of it getting picked up by the Coast Guard, or any other friendly vessel.

The throttle was firewalled, pushing the *Island Girl* with all the power the engines could generate. She hit a flat area of water and shot forward, picking up speed. Jack watched to see if the Cubans were following behind through the patch of calm. The water was flat and the sky had cleared. The light hurt Jack's eyes as he looked in wonder at the towering walls of turbulence rising high into the sky all around him — *the eye of the storm.* Jack judged that the eye must have been a half- mile across and pointed the boat back on course — due north. He surveyed the boat and was amazed they were still afloat. The decompression chamber was lodged tight at an angle, the transom gone, the port gunnels gone, and the port windscreen smashed. The bow looked like a giant shark had bitten the *Girl's* nose off. Large chunks of decking were chewed up from the Cuban's deck gun … a .50 caliber from the looks of the holes. Heavy smoke was spiraling out of the engine room.

"Everybody topside … *Now!*" Jack yelled. "Come on, move it, move it! This is our chance to get ready to abandon ship."

The two Michaels peeked out of the hatch, then came up on to deck. Junior was next, then Tommy. It was the most pitiful looking crew that ever went to sea. Junior was doubled over in pain, his front side soaked in blood. Big Mike was still doubled over, hacking up seawater and phlegm, Little Mike was shaking with fear, and Tommy looked feverish and in pain.

"I'm going to push the engines for as long as she floats, but we need to be ready to go for a swim," Jack said, almost in a normal voice. "I'm not sure exactly where we are, and there's a Cuban gunboat close behind us. We can sit here and wait to be captured or blown out of the water, or we can keep going, knowing at some point soon, we'll have to abandon the boat."

The little knot of men just looked back at Jack without a word, leaving the decision to him.

"OK. Tommy get down in the engine room and hit them with the fire extinguishers and foam, then grab the pot of grease and bring it topside … move it," Jack ordered.

"Big Mike, haul that line in and tie Junior and Little Mike to it in three or four foot intervals, then tie yourself in. Make sure you cut the end off the bow cleat. Tie them tight. That's going to be our life line."

Jack noticed that the smoke from the engine room had stopped billowing out at the same time the port engine stopped. When he hit the ignition, there was no response. He tried again. Dead, no juice. Jack centered the port throttle and watched the heat gauge on the starboard start to rise. Time was running out.

Tommy rushed back topside carrying a paint bucket of heavy grease that he used on the bearings and moving parts.

"Slather up Little Mike first, head to foot. He'll be the first to get cold," Jack yelled as he concentrated on his gauges.

Tommy scooped a handful of the grease out of the bucket and plopped it on Mike's head with a smile. Two minutes later, Little Mike looked like the Tar Baby. His eyes were wide, and his smile toothy. Big Mike saw what was to be done and started on himself.

"Don't put that shit on me, Tommy. You take it. I'm a dead man here," Junior groaned.

"Bullshit, you're doing fine. Now sit still while I feel you up."

"I know I'm fine, that ain't what I'm saying. Look over there, what do you see?" Junior asked.

Tommy took a quick look over his shoulder, "Nothing, just water."

"That's what I'm saying. The money, it's going down with the ship. So what am I supposed to tell the Don, I ask you? We hit a fucking iceberg?" Junior said, looking tortured.

Jack was listening to the back and forth and smiled at Junior's supposed predicament with the Don. If they lived over the next few hours, it would be a miracle. The Don should be the least of Junior's worries.

"Tommy, when you finish up with the grease, give me the pot and bring up all the life vests along with anything that will float and tie it off to the line. Grab all the jerky that's left, too. I think we're going to need it." Jack looked over at Junior, who had his eyes shut tight in pain. "Make sure you get Junior tied in good and tight."

Soon, everyone was tied off to the safety line except Jack who was still at the helm. They had a hundred yards to go before they hit the north wall of the hurricane, then they would be back in the storm. Jack was sick with worry knowing that the worst was yet to come. Hurricanes rotate counterclockwise, and the east wall is the deadliest. What they had been through for the past several hours was the weak side. Things were going to get very serious in just a few minutes. He shuddered.

The assault from the storm on the small boat was terrifying. Nothing had ever prepared anyone for the violence that hit them. Just the wind alone tried to pull the boat out of the water and hurl it skyward. At one moment, the bow was almost completely vertical, with everyone grabbing at anything they could just to stay aboard. Little Mike was whisked overboard, then pulled back by Tommy and his father, hauling with all their strength. Without the lifeline, he would have disappeared forever. The boat was suddenly in the air, spinning, turning, then just as suddenly, smacked back down, knocking one of the engines off its mount sending it crashing through the hull. The hull was flooded in seconds.

Little Mike and Big Mike were in the water, Junior was up on his knees starting to dog paddle, and Tommy was taking a last look at his drowning love. Jack had strapped a diving vest to the windshield frame earlier as a precaution that, if all electronics went out, he would at least have the low frequency pulse tone that a diver could activate on his buoyancy compensator if he got in trouble on the bottom. The low frequency could be picked up by sonar and guide a rescue team to them. The responder life was advertised to be forty-eight hours. Jack had never had to use one so wasn't really sure if he should have even bothered. Forty-eight hours from now they would either be dead or out in the Caribbean Sea somewhere. Nevertheless, he punched the sealed rubber activator and joined Tommy at the stern.

"This is it, Tommy," Jack yelled into his friend's ear as they both stepped off the submerging deck, directly into the turbulent water.

The string of men was separated by a few feet of nylon line between each person. Tommy had tied off all of the extra life vests between the men, the line looking more like a fat kite's tail with men tied to it strung out behind the sinking boat than a lifeline. The *Island Girl* slipped under, leaving nothing behind. Each of the men were so busy trying to keep their heads above water that they missed her passing, sinking fast towards the bottom, a hundred feet below. Suddenly, Jack was pulled under water with a mighty force. He was confused and ready to panic. He didn't have any air in his lungs, and he could feel pressure building on his ears as he was pulled deeper. It came to him in a flash that Big Mike hadn't untied the other end of the lifeline from the front cleat. The line was still tied to the boat and was pulling them all down to their deaths. Jack found the line with his hand and searched for his K-bar knife with the other. He needed to cut the line now or all five of them would be dead in minutes. He held the blade to the taut line and yanked, immediately his body shot upward, pulled by all the buoyant life vests. He passed each of the men on his way up and was the first to break the surface, where he gulped huge mouthfuls of air, then gagged when saltwater filled his mouth.

Each head popped up to the surface, coughing and spluttering, except for Big Mike. His head sagged at an odd angle and bobbed crazily. Tommy grabbed him and pulled him close. The nylon lifeline had somehow circled Michael's neck, snapping it when he was jerked by the force of the sinking boat. Little Mike saw his father's head wallowing back and forth and knew something terrible had happened. He shut his eyes tight and held his fists to his eyes so he wouldn't have to see. He didn't want to know. Too much had already happened in his young life and he knew he couldn't handle any more.

Time became meaningless, hour after hour of relentless motion as the string of men bobbed, and sank, surfaced, and were thrown and whipped around. Their tongues and mouths were eaten raw by the saltwater, their eyes were burning orbs, their skin puckered, and parted in hundreds of little cuts from the abrasion of the salt. The grease coating had been quickly eaten away, exposing flesh, bringing their body temperatures down. The wind and the rain worked together to torment the men as they were carried by the storm in some unknown direction. Periods of unconsciousness grew longer as their equilibriums gave up the fight to understand what was happening to their world of up and down. The men rode atop the bucking waves, near death — time meant nothing.

Chapter 12

The wind from the storm slammed the shed with wrecking ball blows, tearing a corrugated panel from the roof, spinning it off into the maelstrom. Agent Olsen rolled up in a ball as a wall of stacked cases of empty bottles crashed down, breaking and shattering, cutting and stabbing as they hit him and the floor. Tiny, Ike's babysitting German shepherd, was up and scratching at the locked door. With every flash of lightning and boom of thunder, Tiny howled in fear. *Some killer,* Olsen thought. Olsen searched around to find a shard of glass to use on the zip lock binding his hands behind him. A sharp pain dug into his hand from a shattered bottle neck. It bled, making his hand slippery as he started to saw at the binding. It didn't take long to free his hands, tear the duct tape off his eyes and mouth with a quick painful yank, and then free his feet. Tiny turned and saw his prisoner standing and hunched up, ready to pounce, when a tremendous burst of wind blew two of the walls out and away. Tiny let out a yelp and disappeared into the dark. Olsen was drenched in seconds as he hunted around for the shovel he had spotted in the shed moments before. The backdoor hinges to Ike's Bar popped off effortlessly as he used the shovel blade as a lever between the hasps and the old wood frame. Once inside the bar, Olsen found the stainless sink and wrapped his mouth around the faucet and sucked in water, took a breath, and sucked in more. The only light came from a neon beer sign over the back wall and a hanging light over a pool table that was swinging ominously from the wind blowing through the eaves. Olsen washed up in the bar sink as he tried to figure out where he was. A printed bar napkin read 'Ike's Old Town Juke.' It didn't mean anything to Olsen as he toweled his face and neck. In a back room, he found an old Walther P38 in a desk drawer. Next to it was an envelope with a couple hundred bucks in small bills inside. Olsen shoved the money in his pocket and the pistol in his waistband. The storm was blowing hard, shaking the frame building, making the hundred-year-old clapboards moan and groan as if in pain as it swayed perilously.

Olsen slammed the office phone down in its cradle when he didn't get a dial tone. Then, in a fit of frustration, he threw the phone against a cabinet, breaking the glass front, showering the floor with splinters of glass. A pay phone hung on the wall across from the restroom. Olsen snatched it up and was surprised when he heard a dial tone. *'Good Old Dixie Bell,'* Olsen thought as he searched his pockets for change, coming up with a dime. The coin tray in the bar's cash register was filled with enough change to call China. Olsen scooped out a handful of quarters and went back to the hallway.

"You have reached DEA's Miami office. Our office hours are 9 A.M to 6 P.M. every day except Saturday and Sunday. If this is an emergency please dial 911, Thank you for calling the Miami DEA office." Click.

"Fucking government workers," Olsen said frustrated. "Bastards even took my quarter." He put another coin in and asked the operator to connect him to the Monroe County Sheriff's Office.

"Monroe Sheriff's Office, Sergeant Clyde speaking."

"Sgt. Clyde, this is an emergency. I need to speak with Sheriff Perry."

"State your name and purpose of call."

"DEA Special Agent Jim Olsen. I'm working with the Sheriff on the cartel drug murders."

"10-6, standby."

Olsen stood listening to the storm beating against the building, wondering if it was going to blow away before he got out of it.

"Agent Olsen, the Sheriff has asked for your 10-7 location, and wants you to remain there. He is sending a unit to pick you up," the dispatcher said.

"Tell him to hurry, this dump is about to collapse around me."

Olsen was standing behind the bar eating a handful of mixed nuts when the electricity blew, throwing the room into a blackness so dense that he couldn't even see his hands. The wind howling through the eaves and cracks sent chills up his back and neck as he subconsciously pulled the Walther out from his waistband and checked the action, ensuring a round was in the chamber. As his eyes became accustomed to the dark, he relaxed a little and placed the pistol on the bar top while he wiped his face again with a wet bar towel. A crash from the hallway startled him as the back door flew open and a streaking object hit him solidly in the chest, knocking him back against the back bar, smashing glasses, shelving, bottles of whiskey, and wine. Olsen covered his head as teeth sunk into his shoulder, just missing his jugular by a few centimeters. The German shepherd shook its head violently back and forth, trying to rip flesh out as it growled and snarled in a primal rage. Olsen was shocked by the ferocity of the big dog's attack and tried to push it away from him, but couldn't break the dog's grip. The more he tried to break away, the more intense the dog's fury. The bar was the only reason Olsen was still erect as the dog reset its teeth, taking in more flesh as it continued snapping and shaking its head violently. Olsen's mind was still in its initial shock, but he knew the dog would win if he didn't do something to get away. One hand was searching the bar top for the Walther as the other hand tried to break the dog's hold. As the dog chewed the shoulder and neck area, it also had its back legs furiously clawing and digging into Olsen's chest and abdomen. Olsen was desperate, he couldn't find the pistol and the pain was almost unbearable. The dog was just too powerful and was going to win if he didn't do something. Olsen instinctively grabbed the dog's balls and squeezed, jerking hard at the same time. He wanted to pull the fucking things off if he could, and jerked even harder. The big dog let go of its hold and howled painfully. Olsen pushed the dog back with his elbow, grabbed its head and smashed it as hard as he could against the bar. A flash of lightning lit up the bar. Olsen spotted and grabbed the pistol, placing the barrel against the dog's chest and fired. The dog yelped loudly and Olsen shot it again. The dog whimpered as it crumbled to the floor, gasping for air. Olsen kicked hard and fired a round into its head, then collapsed next to it.

Olsen knew he was injured badly. The blood flowing from his abdomen was like liquid fire as it pooled in his lap, and the torn flesh on his shoulder felt like ground meat and throbbed painfully to the touch. This wasn't looking too good for him. Unless the patrol car arrived soon and got him to a hospital, he wasn't going to make it out of this dump. He tried to stand up and make his way to the wall phone but collapsed back down with pain and shock when he saw a large piece of intestine hanging out just below his navel. His first thought was that if he moved, the intestine would slide out even more, just like the training films in Basic taught him. He also knew to keep the exposed part wet until he could be treated. He groped around and found the towel that he had used to clean up with and placed it gently on the wound. Suddenly, a bright light flashed on his face, blinding him.

"What you doing down there, Agent Olsen?" Sheriff Perry asked as he held the flashlight steady on Olsen's face.

"Thank God, Sheriff. I need to get to a hospital now. My gut's cut open and I'm losing blood," Olsen pleaded.

"That dog do all that slicin' and dicin'? Lordy, you're a mess, Special Agent," Perry said as he squatted down, shining the light on Olsen's wounds. "I'd say you got yourself into some deep shit here, and I'm trying to figure out how you're going to get yourself out of this mess."

"Sheriff, we need to move it. I need help now. Let's chitchat later, all right?"

"Well, these things take time to figure out, Mr. DEA Man-From-Miami. Us little people down here at the county level like to dicker with folks from up on the mainland, you see," the Sheriff said in his best campaign folksy tone. "The way I see it, you have something that belongs to me, and I have your ride to the hospital sittin' out front, motor running, just waiting."

"What the fuck are you talking about?" Olsen said, faking puzzlement.

"Yeah, I want to know everything you've done since Gomez whipped your ass the other night. You told him you were hot on the trail of where the money was. What was your plan, take it all and run with it without even a neighborly goodbye, Partner?"

"I don't know where it is, Perry," Olsen lied, immediately on the defense.

"You and I both know you're lying, so knock off the crap and tell me what you've found out about where the ten million bucks is," Perry demanded as he poked his pistol into Olsen's stomach wound. "The sooner you tell me what I want to hear, the sooner we'll get you some help."

It didn't take Olsen long to figure out the game Perry was playing. He either went along with the Sheriff, or he died.

"Ok, fair enough, but first get me to the hospital."

"Nope, can't do it that way. You fed boys cheat. I want you to tell me where the money is or who has it, then we'll scoot on over to the E.R."

Olsen was getting weaker by the minute from blood loss and was having a hard time focusing his thoughts. His mind flashed to a photograph of his wife and two daughters that sat on his desk in Miami. How did it come down to this, he thought?

"Jack Marsh and his partner Tommy Hicks have the money. Yesterday, or before the storm started, they had the money in a rental storage space at the Keys Storage. The last I saw of them, they were either loading or unloading garbage bags of money, I'm not sure which. They hit me with a stun gun and knocked me out. The next thing I know, I was tied up on the floor of the storage room that used to sit behind this shit hole bar," he gasped for breath, and spit up blood. "The money might still be in the rental space, or maybe around here somewhere. Some broad named Black Alice is involved somehow, too, but I don't know what the connection is." Olsen fell silent and let his chin droop to his chest to rest for a moment.

Sheriff Perry thought through everything he was just told, looking for any missing parts or links back to him, "Olsen, wake up. What's the storage number, and where's your car?"

"Storage number … uh, I can't remember, 2 something … 261, yeah, 261 that's it. Last I saw of my car, it was sitting in front of the space. Let's go, Sheriff. I'm just about bled out."

Sheriff Perry placed his pistol barrel on the crown of Olsen's head and fired, killing him instantly. Olsen's body slumped back across the dead dog, trembled for a couple of seconds, then laid still.

"Who's in there? Come on out," a voice called from the back door. Lightning flashed and silhouetted a big man standing in the frame holding a rifle of some kind.

"Sheriff Perry, police business. Drop that weapon and place your hands on your head," the Sheriff commanded.

"Don't shoot, Sheriff; it's me, Ike Jones. This is my place," Ike said, as he leaned his shotgun against the wall and placed his hands on his head.

"Walk forward, Mr. Jones. Nice and slow, any fast moves and I'll shoot."

"Naw sir, I'm not trying nuthin'. I just come down here to check on my place in this storm and thought I heard a gunshot go off."

"Put your hands on the bar, so I can see them," Perry demanded.

Ike placed his hands flat on the bar and Perry had cuffs on him before he could react.

"What's going on here? I didn't do nothing. This is my place …"

Perry hit Ike across the jaw with the butt of his pistol and shoved him down onto the floor.

"You're under arrest for the murder of a DEA Agent, Mr. Jones. I'll tell you right now, you don't have any rights, so don't expect me to be reciting any of that politically correct crap either," Sheriff Perry snarled.

"What the fuck, man? This is my place, I ain't killed nobody …"

"Shut up, *boy*. I'm dragging you in for murder, kidnapping, false imprisonment, and God knows what else."

"Sheriff, I ain't done none of those things, I swear," Ike pleaded.

"I told you to shut up. DEA Agent Olsen here told me before you shot him that you and Jack Marsh hid some bags of money around here. Now, you tell me where it is you got it hidden and I'll see if I can't spare you some of them charges … but not all of 'em." Perry was fishing for information.

"Jack Marsh came here yesterday and asked could I hold a bag of money for him and keep some white man tied up until he got back, that's all. That dead man lying on the floor over there looks like the man he brought in, but I don't know how he got in here or how he got himself shot," Ike said, scared out of his mind.

"What about the money he asked you to hold for him? Where is it?"

"It's in that trash can under the bar over there. One can's got beer cans in it, and the other has that bag of money he left for me. He said he'd kill me if I told anybody, Sheriff. I been scared out of my wits all day and night, then this storm blows in and my business is ruined. I don't know what I'm going to do now." Ike was crying, more for effect than out of concern for his business.

Perry stepped over the dog and Olsen and flashed his light on a green bag stuffed in the trash can. He quickly tore open the bag and smiled when he saw the money packed inside. He ran a hand down deep into the bag and pulled out a handful of hundred dollar bills and let them flutter through his fingers, smiling. He tied off the top of the bag and tossed it on the other side of the bar. His heart was beating fast as he smiled, thinking that if he played this right he could end up with all the drug money *and* get rid of the spic Gomez at the same time.

"Is that rifle loaded out there in the hallway?" Perry asked Ike as he passed by him.

"Yes sir, that's a shotgun and she's loaded. Be careful, that trigger is mighty sharp," Ike said.

Perry retrieved the shotgun and returned to the bar.

"On your feet, Jones," the Sheriff commanded.

"Where we going?"

"Over to the office to be booked," Perry answered as he led Ike behind the bar, for some reason facing Olsen and the dog.

Once he had Ike positioned where he wanted him, he squatted down next to Olsen and pointed the shotgun up at an angle towards Ike's chest and fired. The heavy buckshot load lifted Ike off his feet and threw him back against the wall, tearing his chest open. Ike slid down the wall leaving a blood trail as he went, a look of horror frozen on his face. Perry wiped the shotgun down with the bloody bar towel Olsen had used before he died, and then put the shotgun in Olsen's grip, placing the index finger on the trigger. Perry picked up the

Walther from the floor, hopped up on the bar and swung himself over, knocking a bar stool over as he landed. Careful not to step in any blood, he placed the Walther in Ike's hand and backed away from the bar. As he stood surveying the crime scene that he had created, he felt confident that the CSI boys would agree that Ike probably surprised someone he thought was a burglar, there was a shootout, and both men were killed. End of investigation.

As Perry moved his flashlight beam over the carnage, the storm raged outside. Inside, the bar smelled of cordite, blood, and whiskey. The working side of the bar was a shamble of broken bottles, bloody walls, and splintered reflections of light off the mirror. One last look around and Perry slung his bag of cash over his shoulder and stepped out into the backspace, shrugging his shoulder up tight to keep the rain from running down his neck. He ran down the side alley out to the street, hurried over to the patrol car idling with windshield wipers slapping, and headlights cutting through the rain. "Let's roll, Sergeant," he called out to Sgt. Short, who sat behind the wheel looking worried and not understanding the situation.

Olsen tossed the bag of money in the caged backseat and jumped in the shotgun seat. "I said roll, damn it. Let's move it."

"Is everything okay, Sheriff? You were gone a long time. I was getting ready to send out for help," Short said, stealing a sideways glance at his boss's boss.

"You did good, Short. You did exactly what I told you to do. I like that in a young deputy. You follow orders and keep your mouth shut and it won't be long before you'll be up for some higher rank, son," Perry said, slapping Short on the leg. "Why, I think I'll just reassign you to be my adjutant. What do you say to that, son?"

"Well, I'm pretty happy where I am under Lt. Mathers. If I had a choice, I would stay there and hopefully earn a promotion coming up through homicide."

"Too slow for a boy with your talent. I'll tell you what, you work with me the next few days on this drug money thing, and I'll promote you to lieutenant when we solve the case," Perry said, beaming.

"Well, I don't know what to say, Sheriff ..."

"No need to say anything. You just keep your mouth shut, see what I say to see, and look the other way when I say. That's pretty easy to follow."

"Yes, Sir, I can live with that," Short said, not liking the arrangement at all. *Something happened back there and this guy is trying to shut me up,* he thought.

"Before we go back to the office, run us out to the Keys Storage out past the golf course. I need to check on something."

The gate was wrapped with a chain and combination lock that popped open easy when Sgt. Short snapped the hasp, then pushed the gate open. Back in the car, he wiped his face dry with a wad of paper towels off a roll and pulled forward.

"We're looking for unit 261," Sheriff Perry said as he flashed the unit's spotlight at the unit numbers as they rolled down the aisle.

"Hold up, there it is. Jump out and pop the lock then come back to the car. I'll go inside alone in case there's any danger," Perry said.

Perry was disappointed when he raised the overhead door and found Olsen's sedan inside. There were no bags of money as he had hoped, only a piece of crap fed plain wrap unit. He pulled the overhead down and ran back to the unit. Inside, he sat for a moment thinking of what to do next.

"Young Sergeant, I think I know who our killer is." Perry announced.

"Who?" Short was taken aback by this statement.

"Jack Marsh. Marsh is our killer."

Chapter 13

The first thing Jack tried to comprehend as he became aware, was the quiet that surrounded him. He squinted through salt-crusted eyes and threw up bile. He was almost motionless as he floated in calm water. The rain had stopped, the storm nothing more than gray overhead. His mind was playing tricks, thinking it was still being tossed around. Jack's deck shoes were gone, his pistol belt with his pistol and knife were gone, his neck was raw, flesh exposed from the life vest rubbing against it for hours, his hands so puckered and sore that he couldn't close them. His stomach and gut were cramped painfully from all the salt water he had swallowed, but he was alive.

Tommy was awake and holding Little Mike close to him trying to keep them both warm. Their teeth were chattering loudly. Little Mike had his arms around Tommy's neck and his head on his shoulder, in a stupor. Big Mike was gone. Junior had pulled himself up onto a half dozen of the extra life vests and was snoring as he floated. Jack pulled himself over to Junior to check his wound and saw that it had turned black around the ragged edges with bloody pus seeping out of it. Jack's first thought was that gangrene was forming. He put his nose down close to the hole to get a whiff and pulled away from the putrid smell.

"Tommy, how are you and Mike?"

Tommy floated for a few seconds in a daze, trying to organize his thoughts, and then turned his attention back to Little Mike, ignoring Jack, and pulling the child closer into him in a tight embrace.

As the hours slipped by, the seas became calm and flat. The sky cleared to a brilliant blue and the sun scorched the floating men as the Gulf Stream carried them north at a constant three knots per hour. Minutes seemed like hours as the sun made its run across the sky. Towards dusk, a pod of curious dolphins nosed up to the floating men, sticking their noses up against the life vests and men, jabbering excitedly among themselves. One of the larger dolphins surfaced close to Little Mike and spoke soft *bleeps* and *thleeps* as it shook its head up and down and submerged, only to pop back up closer and spit water on Tommy and Little Mike. Then it was gone again with a loud bleep and a splash of its tail.

As the sun slid below the western horizon, stars began blinking overhead. Off to the east, a sliver of moon was starting its nightly run across the sky, bringing a slight breeze with it that chilled the sunburned men. Jack went to each vest and activated the small pulse light to attract any passing ships or anyone out looking for them. At first, Jack was worried that the light might attract sharks, but his concern about being found outweighed the risk of being eaten by sharks. He also knew that the shipping routes up from the Panama Canal and the large petroleum refineries from Houston and Mobile ran parallel to the Gulf Stream, and there was a good chance that they would be picked up by one of these tankers if they were seen.

Overhead, the sky became a ceiling of glittering diamonds, rubies, and emeralds as the stars revealed themselves, uncaring and unconcerned about the men floating in the black sea below. The moon was just as unfriendly as it slowly slid across the sky. Jack shortened the lifeline so that the men would be closer together to share body heat, as well as for safety. Night on the open water could be a terrifying experience if you let your imagination get away from you. Knowing there were hundreds of feet of water below you and any number of creatures that would love to nibble on toes, fingers, or a nice bloody ribcage had a way of instilling fear in one's mind.

Jack forced himself not to think of those possibilities, and instead tried to recall everything that had happened over the last few days. The mystery that he couldn't answer was why Colonel Carson wanted to kill the crew once he and the team were delivered to their destination. Especially Junior, who supposedly was the Mafia's representative. Don Cona had implied that the Mafia would be back in control of Cuba once Castro was taken out and they had their man in office as president. Miguel Santos supposedly was their man who was going to step in and run things, giving the Mafia carte blanche on the casinos, hotels, and the tourist business. The Don also implied that the U.S. government was his partner, but with different objectives. The political objectives, as far as Jack could figure, were to make the huge island a buffer between the mainland and the expanding socialist countries of South America. Control of Cuba would give the U.S. a necklace of islands running across the Caribbean Sea, protecting its southern underbelly from enemies coming from the sea. Jack also knew that there had been huge fields of oil discovered off western Cuba and that the Chinese had already begun to tap wells almost in sight of the U.S. mainland. Several large U.S.

oil companies had complained to the Department of Energy about China's exploration, alerting the DEA of China's platforms slant-drilling into U.S. territorial waters.

None of this big picture stuff explained why the Colonel was so quick to shoot Tommy and Junior, unless the man really was psycho and meant what he said about wanting the notoriety and the glory of taking Castro down. Also, the relationship between the covert team and the Colonel was not a normal Spec Ops bond that exists in tight units. Jack was sure the Colonel really wasn't a military officer at all, but more likely out of one of the dozen or so agencies that sprang up after 9-1. Jack's mind drifted as he tried to pull it all together. One moment he was talking with Don Carlos, and the next his old man was beating his mother. He slept as the current carried him north into the night.

Chapter 14

Lt. Mathers stood inside Ike's Juke Joint with a handkerchief held to his nose, but still had to breathe through his mouth so he wouldn't vomit from the smell. Key West and Monroe County could be like an old Wild West town at times, but murder scenes like this were a rarity. The strange part of the scene was how perfectly the crime scene could be read in spite of the carnage. Man discovered burglarizing a bar, owner discovers man, shoot-out ensues, men kill each other, case closed. That is, until you look closer and little details popped out that told you something totally different happened to these two men. The first thing Lt. Mathers discovered was that the "burglar" was DEA Agent Jimmy Olsen, who had been working the same case he and his task force were working. The second thing was that Olsen had been shot in the crown of his head, leaving powder burns and singed hair indicating an execution-style tap. The other problem was the location of Ike Jones's body. If he had delivered the pop to Olsen's head, then there was no way that Olsen could have then blown Jones against the far wall. Olsen would have been dead and couldn't have shot Ike.

"Hold everyone outside. I don't want anybody in here until the CSI crew arrives," Mathers instructed the other uniformed men around him.

"What the hell's going on here?" Sheriff Perry yelled as he jumped out of his patrol unit before Sgt. Short came to a complete stop. "Get this place cleaned up and roped off before the damn TV people get here."

"Sheriff, I have everyone standing by until CSI gets here," Mathers said.

The Sheriff didn't even acknowledge Mathers as he brushed by him and entered the bar.

"Mathers, get in here," Perry bellowed out.

As Lt. Mathers and Sgt. Short entered the bar, they saw that the Sheriff was standing over Olsen's body, trying to sit him up.

"Lieutenant, how long you been a Deputy?"

"Fifteen years, Sheriff."

"Fifteen years and you tell me you couldn't figure out what happened in here? That you need some college pansies to tell you what happened? How the hell did you ever make lieutenant?" The Sheriff said sardonically.

"Any rookie out of the academy could tell you this is a straight burglary gone bad. This colored fellow shot that white man and then the white man shot the colored one before he died. Case closed."

"Sheriff, I don't read it that way. I think …"

"I don't give a shit what you think. I said case closed. Now get this place cleaned up before we have the neighborhood rioting over a white man killing a colored," Sheriff Perry said as he stormed out.

Sgt. Short followed the Sheriff out, stopping long enough to make eye contact with Lt. Mathers.

"Watch yourself, Billy, he's dangerous," Mathers whispered.

"You too, Loo."

An hour later, Lt. Mathers sat in his patrol unit and dialed a number at the Florida State Bureau of Investigation in Tallahassee. As he waited for the connection to go through, he watched the last of the cleanup crew finishing up with swabbing and sanitizing the crime scene at Ike's place. The crowd had dwindled down to just a few kids hanging around in hopes of seeing more bodies brought out in body bags. Mathers knew that what he was about to do could backfire on him and cost him his career, possibly his life, if things got bad.

"Captain Price speaking."

"Captain, this is Lt. Mathers, Monroe County Sheriff's Department. You may remember me from a few years back when we worked a kidnapping case here in the Keys together," Mathers said.

"Sure, I remember. The guy that strangled and raped the two little sisters. Yeah, nasty business, that one."

"Well, I have a problem and I don't know where to start. If I'm wrong, I could be out on the street. But if I'm right, I think we have a bad apple that needs picking."

"Well, as they say, start at the beginning, Loo."

After twenty minutes of giving the Captain the background on the murders, missing drug money, and his suspicions about Sheriff Perry, the phone was silent.

"Captain, you still there?" Mathers asked.

"Yeah, I'm here, just jotting down notes."

Another few minutes slipped by, "Lieutenant, tell me again about this guy named Jack Marsh and how you think he is involved in all this."

"I think he was unwittingly sucked in somehow because of his friendship with Wendell Chalmers, the homeless man who was killed. Then later on, I suspect he tried to find who Chalmers's murderer was and got himself mixed up deeper, the closer he got to the missing money. Then, the Sheriff learned something that tied Marsh to everything going on and he determined that Marsh was the killer and had the money."

"All right, Loo. I want you to stand by for about an hour while I talk to a few people, then I'll get back to you. Fair enough?"

"Sure, Captain, just don't fuck me on this. My ass is hanging out in the wind down here, and there's no place to run to."

"Loo, right now I'm the best friend you got," the Captain said and hung up.

Chapter 15

Jack's dream of a dolphin pulling him through the water by his hands as it whistled a high piercing sound seemed too real to be his imagination. His eyes were swollen shut, so he couldn't see what all the clamor was about, but the sensation of being lifted was real. One eye cracked open and he saw that he was clear of the water and was being reeled up into the back ramp of a huge helicopter hovering high above him. Hands grabbed him and pulled him inside as he cleared the ramp. Just as quickly, his clothes were cut off and warm blankets tucked in all around him like a cocoon. He felt a couple of pin pricks to his arm, then someone was wiping his face with a towel and saying something that Jack couldn't understand. The face went away and the helicopter vibrated, dulling Jack's senses and sending him into a deep sleep.

Jack felt nauseated from the constant rocking and back and forth movement, and was surprised when he opened his eyes and found himself tucked in tight to a hospital bed with the sides up so he wouldn't fall out. He didn't know where he was or how he got there. He remembered a little about being lifted into a helicopter, but, beyond that, there was no memory. The nausea in his stomach was intense, and when he belched, a bit of salty bile came up. A curtain was pulled across the room and Jack could hear someone snoring loudly, but couldn't see who it was. He tried to call out for a nurse, but the only thing that came out was a croak and more bile. Frustrated, he closed his eyes and slept.

"Wake it up, big boy, quit playing possum," a nurse said, as she tugged at Jack's big toe. "You can't lie there forever, as much as you'd probably like to. The doctor's making his rounds and will want you awake."

Jack cracked an eye open, "Go away unless you have food," Jack said.

"No food until the doctor says so, Marine," the nurse said as she strutted around the bed cranking up the angle into a reclining position and popping a thermometer in Jack's mouth. Jack focused his eyes and saw that the nurse was a really nice looking redhead with all the right bumps and curves in the right places.

"Why'd you call me, Marine? Is this another nightmare?"

"The tattoo, Jarhead. The U.S.M.C tattoo on your left arm gave it away. I don't know who is worse, you Marines and your U.S.M.C. tattoos, or the Swabbies and their U.S.N. tats," she chuckled. "Now that you're awake, maybe we can find out more about you and notify your people."

"Where am I?" Jack asked.

"Miami V.A. Hospital. You were brought in here two days ago, dehydrated, blistered by the sun, hypothermic, and with a bad case of the trots. Other than that, we don't know a thing about you except your name, rank, and serial number from the national data center," the nurse said frowning. "Somewhere, there has to be someone who is very worried about you."

Jack lay back thinking about this new wrinkle. No one knew where he was. This could be a good thing if any of the

Colonel's boys were looking for him to finish him off, or any of the cartel mutts looking for their money.

"Was anyone else brought in with me?"

"Not here, but two men and a boy are at Jackson Memorial across the street. From what I hear, the men have bullet wounds and the kid has amnesia. All three are in critical condition and still listed as John Does. The police have been hanging around since you arrived to find out about the wounded men and what happened to you guys."

"Everyone's alive then?" Jack said, relief flooding over him.

"Well, if there were only four of you, then I would say that you all made it from wherever you were," the nurse said, eyeing Jack. "Exactly how did you guys get yourselves into such a dangerous situation?"

"It's a long story, ma'am."

"Well, there's a line of people waiting for you to come around so they can ask you that same question … most are from one law agency or another. I can tell by the bulges in their jackets that they're not here to just wish you well," she said in a low voice, nodding her head to the door. "My advice, don't let them in too soon. You're still weak from the last few days so they can wait."

"Thanks, Nurse … What's your name?" Jack asked.

"Trudy, just call me Trudy, Sugar."

"OK Trudy Sugar. Do I have any clothes or something to wear besides this gown? I feel silly wearing this."

"I don't know about that. I think you look pretty hunky from where I'm standing," she said with a wicked smile. "You came in as naked as the day you were born, no clothes, shoes, wallet — nothing. I could probably scare up something from the barrel downstairs. I can't promise it will be the latest fashion statement, but it will be clean."

The door opened and an emaciated man in a doctor's smock came in with a clipboard in one hand and a stethoscope in the other. "Lazarus has risen I see," the man said, holding out his hand to shake. "I'm Doctor Camp. Between Trudy and me, we own you until we have you back on your feet. If Nurse Trudy tells you to do something, or not do something, consider it having come from me," Dr. Camp said as he reversed the handshake and took Jack's pulse. "Other than exposure and dehydration, you are in fairly good shape. I'm thinking a few days pumping fluids in you should have you out of here by the weekend." He added as he flitted from one side of the bed to the other, poking and prodding.

"The question of the hour, of course, is, who you are. It seems like half of South Florida has an interest in you. The only government rep we don't have on the list is the IRS, and I'm sure they'll be jumping to the head of the line once they know that you survived your ordeal at sea, and the TV people are about to have a coronary out there," he said, flipping his head towards the door.

"Doc, I honestly don't remember who I am or how I got here," Jack lied. "I remember being in the water and throwing up a lot, but beyond that, it's all a blank."

Dr. Camp and Trudy exchanged looks. "Well, that is certainly something that could happen from dehydration. The body basically dries up from the inside out, which affects the central nervous system, which, in turn, could cause any number of psychoneurotic symptoms. My guess is that, with hydration, memory will return, but for now, let's go with amnesia."

"Thanks, Dr. Camp," Jack said and relaxed back on his pillow. He wasn't sure why he told the doctor he couldn't remember anything, other than not wanting to talk to the long line of police-types waiting to talk to him out in the hall. Until he knew more, it was best to play dumb.

"I'll be back later today to check on you. Meanwhile, do as Nurse Trudy says," the doctor said, patting Jack on the foot as he and Nurse Trudy left the room.

"Will do, Doc," Jack said to the closed door.

—

Less than thirty seconds later, the door opened and a man in a suit came in and quickly closed the door behind him.

He stuck out his hand to shake, "Captain Price, Florida State Bureau of Investigation. You're Jack Marsh, correct?"

Jack was alarmed at the suddenness of the man coming in the room and without any fanfare, identifying himself ... and Jack.

"I have amnesia. I don't know who I am. Talk to Dr. Camp."

"No need to talk to him. I know who you are, and you're lucky that I got to you first," Price said and sat on the side of the bed. "I am working with Lt. Mathers of the Monroe County Sheriff's Department, trying to unravel all the shit you've got yourself into, Marsh. Do you realize that your life out on the street isn't worth a dime right now?"

"Really, that bad huh?" Jack said, trying not to look nervous.

"Yeah, that bad," Price said flipping open his notebook. "The hospital here ran your prints through the national identification data bank and matched you up within minutes. The only information the hospital could give the Center, besides your prints, was that you had a USMC tattoo on your left shoulder, ergo, you were probably an ex-Marine. Within minutes of the Center announcing that they had a hit, four different agencies responded, requesting more data. I was one of the requesting Agencies and I was on my way down here from Tallahassee within an hour. The other agencies, I'm sure, are close behind, if not already lurking in the hallways. So we need to talk fast and come up with a game plan on what to do next."

"Price, I don't even know you. Why should I tell you anything, assuming that I know something to start with?"

"Knock off the dumb routine, Marsh. Right now there is a warrant for your arrest for two counts of murder in Key West, money laundering, drug dealing, and kidnapping a Federal agent. There's also one pissed-off Sheriff who has already found you guilty, and has told his men to bring you in dead or alive …"

"Sheriff Perry! That son of a bitch says I killed somebody …"

"Yeah, he does think you murdered two men and stole ten million dollars from Señor Gomez, El Condor himself. Lt. Mathers and I believe that the Sheriff is working for Gomez and he's coming after you with guns blazing to get his hands on the money and to shut you up."

"Who else is after me? You said there are several agencies …"

"You stepped into one giant shit sandwich, Marsh, when you agreed to take that Special Operations team to Cuba …"

"Agreed? I didn't agree! I was threatened. I was told that I would be killed if I didn't go along with some kind of plan to drop men off in Cuba with the mission to pop Fidel. I didn't agree at all," Jack spit out.

"I know that, Jack, but something went wrong and the team never accomplished its mission. There hasn't been a peep out of them for five days. According to my sources at the FBI, they were supposed to go in, hit Castro at his mountain retreat, and get back to the beach that night for pickup by sub. Castro is still alive and the team hasn't made any contact back."

"Price, I don't want to know all this stuff. Keep me out of it. I have a hard enough time trying to make a buck selling drinks to a bunch of clowns from the mainland and I know nothing about international assassins or Castro being targeted." Jack pleaded.

"What about your buddy, Don Cona? You think he's just some small time goombah down from Jersey to take the sun? Little Anthony is head of the last of the big organized crime families. He owns half of the people in D.C. and is thought to be the real brain behind this Castro assassination plot. He makes a few calls, pulls a few chains, places stuffed envelopes around D.C., and he has the government falling into line. I would say that he would love to get his hands on you to find out what you know."

"I'm fucked," Jack said nervously. "What's your angle, Price? What do you want from me? You've given me a breakdown of all the others, but what does the F.S.B.I. want me for?"

"Simple. We know you didn't kill anyone and that you were coerced by Don Cona to drop the team off in Cuba. The Don's hit man, Junior Miola, was supposed to go ashore with the Spec Ops boys. He was supposed to stay behind on the Island and pull the Mafia's sleepers together whom the Don had put in place over the last few months, and then await the Don's triumphant entrance once the new Presidente was installed." Price stopped talking so Jack could digest everything he had just been told.

"But forgetting the big national picture, I would say your biggest immediate problems are Sheriff Perry and Gomez. Word on the street is still buzzing about the missing ten million bucks, and Lt. Mathers knows from an inside source that Perry has told Gomez you are the one with the money."

"Price, there is no way I'm going to just sit around here waiting for someone to walk through that door and pop me … even if I could remember anything," Jack said coyly, then snickered at his attempt to be clever.

"Look, Price, tell me what I need to do to get out of this mess. I'm ready to go along with whatever your plan is."

"Sit tight, I need to make a couple of calls, then I'll be back to get you out of here," Price said, getting up and heading for the door.

Nurse Trudy bumped into Price on his way out and quickly closed the door behind her as a camera flash went off behind her.

"Well, the world knows you're awake and they all want to come in for a photo op," Trudy said as she dumped an armload of clothing on the foot of the bed. "Pick through these to see if there's anything that might fit."

"Trudy, I need to get out of here. I don't know what all you've heard or been told, but none of it's true. I'm caught in the middle of a huge fuck-up and if I don't move fast, I'll be dead before the hour's up," Jack said as he rummaged through the clothing and pulled out jeans and a polo shirt.

"Look, Sugar, I'm just a nurse. I only know enemas, blood pressures, and temps. Beyond that, I don't know or see nothing. What I do know, is that I have three teenagers at home who I have to feed and be mom and pop to, so I need this job. Now, if you want to leave, I can't stop you, but I also can't help you. You understand, Mr. Marsh?"

"Trudy, the last thing I want to do is to get you into any trouble, believe me. I just need you to unhook this IV and then go make your rounds, okay?"

Trudy zipped the tape off Jack's arm, taking all the hair along with it, and quickly took out the IV needle.

"Now, if I were the one trying to get out of here, I would probably go through the bathroom, into the adjoining room, and duck out that door," Trudy said as she put a Band-Aid over the IV puncture in Jack's arm. "I'll bet if you time it right, there will be a nurse with a wheelchair waiting to take you down to the ground floor," she said matter-of-factly.

Jack squeezed Trudy's hand, filled with gratitude, "You come down to Key West and I'll feed you the best burger basket on the island …"

"Burger basket! You're going to feed me a lot more than a burger basket, mister," Trudy said. They both laughed.

Jack lodged the guest chair against the door and pulled on the clothes he had picked out of the pile. He pulled the curtain back and saw that his roommate was still snoring away with several IV drips stuck in him. Jack checked the man's small nightstand and emptied the cash out of the wallet, stuffed the guy's cell phone into his pocket, and slipped into his shoes.

"Thanks bro, I'll pay you back," Jack said softly as he maneuvered the beds and IV's around, finally positioning the unconscious man where Jack had been and then pushing the empty bed by the window. Jack fluffed up pillows and pulled the sheets and blanket up over the pillows. The charade wouldn't last long, but every second Jack had ahead of his pursuers would help.

Trudy was waiting with a wheel chair in the adjoining room, and quickly tucked blankets over and around Jack, disguising him as an invalid. Jack sat slumped forward as

Trudy opened the room door and pushed the chair out into the hall. A crowd of waiting paparazzi and government *suits* were standing around talking on cell phones or checking pagers and didn't give the nurse and the sick man being wheeled down the hall a second look.

Once they were alone in the elevator, Jack tore off the blankets and stood up, straightening his clothes out and running a hand through his hair. He reached over and hit the floor button for the fourth floor. "This is where you get off, Trudy," Jack said, giving her a quick hug and a kiss on the cheek.

Chapter 16

The elevator door opened and Trudy rolled the chair out as several people stepped around her to get in. Jack saw a tear rolling down her cheek and promised himself that he would make it up to her. As the door was closing, she turned and blew a kiss, then smiled. On the ground floor, Jack stuck with the crowd as they all went through the lobby and out to the portico. The evening was pleasant but humid. An afternoon shower had cooled things down and the well-kept gardens on either side of the walkway leading to the bus stand smelled fragrant and tropical. Jack stood off to the side of the bus stand's canopy and checked the cell phone for service. *Bingo,* he was in business.

"Yes," Coco answered on the second ring.

"It's me, Jack."

"*Jack!* Is it really you? You're not dead? Oh my God, thank you, thank you," Coco cried.

"It's me and I'm alive. In trouble, but alive," Jack laughed.

"We've been so worried, Jack. We thought you and Tommy were lost in the hurricane. Mimi hasn't stopped crying since the storm. She won't leave the Dive Shack, hoping that Tommy will pull in at any time in *Island Girl*," Coco related excitedly. "The bar is closed off as a crime scene and the Sheriff's thugs broke everything — tables, chairs, all our inventory, everything, Jack," Coco cried.

"Take it easy. We'll be all right, I promise. I just need to get everything straightened out," Jack said. Tell Mimi that Tommy is in Jackson Memorial across from the V.A. Hospital under a John Doe. Tell her to stay away until we figure out our next moves," Jack said as he continued to look around. "I need for you to rent a car and come pick me up. I'm in Miami on the run, so make it as fast as you can."

"I can leave now. I rented a car a couple of days ago so I could get around and stay on top of things. Where should I meet you?"

As Jack was talking, he spotted a Monroe County Sheriff's unit pull in under the portico of the hospital, and stop. Jack could see Sheriff Perry sitting shotgun, talking on the unit radio. Jack ducked as Perry's head swung towards the bus stand and lingered as he studied each face, then moved on to the next one in line. Jack hunkered down with his back to the Sheriff.

"Meet me in the lobby of the Four Seasons at eleven. I want as many people around me as possible until you get there. Don't park, just pull in and I'll come out," Jack instructed. "Before you leave, I need you to do something for me. Go to the bar and inside the walk-in reefer in the right hand ceiling is a false panel. I want you to lift it up, inside there are two bundles of money. Bring me one of the bundles …"

"But, Jack, the Sheriff has the place roped off. I know he has patrol cars checking on the place every so often. I'm scared."

"No problem. Get Lamont to go in and get it for you while you wait down the street. He can slip in and out quicker than you can."

"Okay, we'll do it. I'll see you at eleven sharp."

Jack flipped the phone closed and stole a look over his shoulder as he headed for the canopy to wait with the other vets. Perry was looking closely at the men, slapping the dashboard as he continued talking on the handset. Several men in police and security uniforms pushed out of the hospital's reception area, looking around anxiously.

A light rain had started to fall and the crowd of down-and-out Veterans was bunched up, trying to stay dry while waiting for the downtown bus. Jack had heard that on stormy nights, many of the homeless Vets would spend the night in the emergency room under some pretense of being sick and needing help. Jack thought that they did indeed need help, from neglect more so than imagined physical maladies. Jack turned down an old fellow who offered him a drink out of a bottle in a paper bag. The old man took a big swallow and belched a rancid cheap wine smell.

"S'cuse me, left my manners in the Nam," the guy slurred.

"Hey, no problem, buddy," Jack said as he tried to move away from the wine cloud and still watch the policemen.

"Damn bro, what happened to your face? Willy Pete rounds?" the wino asked, squinting at Jack's face. "That white phosphorous is some bad stuff, I shit you not. Were you up by Hue?"

"Naw, that was way before my time. I was in Kuwait," Jack said.

"Kuwait was for pussies, the real war was the Nam, man," the old vet said and moved on.

Ducking his head low, Jack put his hand up to his face feeling the week old beard and the scabby blisters from the sun and sea. He caught a look of himself in the Plexiglas windscreen of the bus stand and winced. He had a bad case of bed-head, his face looked medium rare, and his arms were bubbled with blisters. If he was lucky, the Sheriff wouldn't recognize him.

"Here she comes," someone said as the men automatically started lining up in an orderly fashion.

Jack was the fifth man in line and had his stolen money folded up in his hand. Two men ahead of him didn't have the right amount and the driver made them step down.

"How much is the fare?" Jack asked.

"Buck-fifty, buddy, if you don't have it, step off the bus," the driver said, bored with the whole process, *night after night, same shit.*

"Here take whatever you need to get all these men on the bus, anything left over keep, buy yourself some respect for these troopers, asshole," Jack said, trying to hurry the loading process.

Five minutes later, the bus was rolling towards downtown. From the back of the bus a slurred voice started singing *Anchors Aweigh*, then a couple more voices chimed in with the Air Force anthem, then an Airborne Ranger cadence. Soon the din was deafening as each branch of service tried to out sing the others.

Someone shouted out, "Let's give a Hoorah to the Skipper for the free ride."

Thirty-five voices gave out three loud *HoooRahh's,* followed by catcalls and whistles.

It all reminded Jack of his early days in the Corps as a young private riding the midnight Vomit Comet from Oceanside back out to Camp Pendleton with all the young Marines drunk, the bus rocking perilously from side to side, and all singing the Marine Corps hymn. Some of the guys just never moved beyond that, Jack thought, as he looked around at the walking wounded.

The bus pulled over and stopped when a police unit cut it off with emergency lights flashing and siren screaming. Jack's blood turned cold, then hot, as adrenaline raced through his system. He was caught. Sheriff Perry and Sgt. Billy Short stepped up on the bus with pistols drawn, alert for trouble. Jack couldn't understand what he was seeing, Billy was his friend. What was he doing with Perry?

"Marsh," Sheriff Perry shouted when he spotted Jack. "You're under arrest. Step off the bus."

Jack had never felt so low as he stood and started for the front of the bus. As Jack got close, Sheriff Perry slapped his pistol across Jack's jaw, knocking him to his knees. Just as quickly, Billy had cuffs on Jack and was trying to stand him up. Up to this point, the men on the bus were silent, but when Jack went down, they all started shouting and yelling. Perry pointed his pistol at the men, "Stand down. This man is wanted for murder. You don't want to interfere." Perry shouted.

The bus fell quiet again as the men sat back in their seats, intimidated by the big fat man with the gun and badge.

"We're all murderers on this ride, Sheriff," a lone voice called out from the back of the bus.

Billy shoved Jack hard against the trunk of the patrol car and kicked his legs apart as he began his pat-down, "You got anything sharp in those pockets Marsh? Anything that will stick me …"

"Step aside, Billy," Sheriff Perry said as he stepped forward and hit Jack on the back of the head with his pistol.

Jack collapsed to the wet street, unconscious.

"Grab his legs and let's throw him in the trunk," Perry said.

"But, Sheriff …"

"Don't 'But Sheriff' me. Grab his legs. Let's get him tucked in before some do-gooders think we're doing police brutality on him."

Perry slammed the trunk down hard and got in behind the wheel.

"I'm driving. You sit there and look pretty, Sgt. Short. We're going to make a little detour before we head for the barn," Perry said, looking over at Short. "Remember, I said if you play your cards right, you'll make lieutenant? Well, you're about to earn your silver bars. I'm going to introduce you to a guy who will make your life a lot easier than it is on a lousy deputy's pay. You ready for a life changer, son?"

"Yes sir. I could use a little sunshine in my life. Who are we going to see?"

"You'll see soon enough."

When the Sheriff turned off Brickell Avenue onto the Rickenbacker Causeway leading out to Key Biscayne, Short knew he was about to meet El Condor himself, the murderous drug dealer, Gomez. A chill of fear ran up his back knowing that he would be watched closely as a newcomer to the gangster's inner circle. He would have to put on the best performance of his life.

Chapter 17

Perry pulled off Harbor Drive into a gated driveway and flashed his lights. A man with an Uzi stepped out of the guard shack and looked closely inside the car, "Señor Gomez was not expecting visitors tonight, Jefe. Uno momento, wait one minute while I tell him you are here," the man said as he brought a small two-way to his mouth, spoke rapidly, listened a moment, and came back to the car.

"Please, Señor, Gomez says to go straight in. Someone will meet you at the door," the man said, waving them through.

"Let me do all the talking. You keep quiet," Perry said as he drove up the drive and parked. "Gomez can smell fear on a man and he'll kill you if he thinks you're lying to him. So it's best to just keep your mouth shut."

Two men with automatic weapons were waiting at the front walk and escorted them inside the Condor's mansion. Short was rubbernecking at the mix of gold gilded walls and red velvet tapestries where huge oversized frames held paintings of nudes, matadors, and mustachioed patriarchs in nineteenth century suits looking down their Spanish aristocratic noses at the two uniformed gringos.

"So, you like my taste in art?" Gomez asked as he approached his two guests.

Two more men, built for trouble, accompanied the Condor. One of the men carried a cattle prod, the other a foot long sandwich.

"Yes sir. I'm especially interested in the oils of your ancestors," Short said.

"Those guys? They are not my ancestors. I took those from a man who owed me money. I like the frames. They are big and look like they cost a lot of money."

"Yeah, I can see how that would work," Short said, catching the Sheriff signaling him to shut up.

"Sheriff Perry, I am glad to see you. Your presence means we have good news about my missing money, no?" Gomez said as he led the group into a large den.

"Better than that. I have the man who has your money, Gomez. I thought you might want to talk to him yourself about it," Perry said.

"You have him? You have the hombre who stole my money and has caused me so much trouble? Please don't joke, Señor. I am in no mood for the jokes."

"Yeah, I have him, but first we need to talk about a finder's fee," Perry said through squinted eyes, as he rubbed his thumbs and fingers together. "I'm not greedy, but you understand I have had to go through a lot of trouble to bring him to you."

"Trouble, Señor Sheriff? I will tell you trouble. I had to pay Don Vargas in Vera Cruz ten million dollars out of my own money to cover what was stolen from me. Then Señor Vargas charged me another two million for being late delivering the money to his people in Cuba. So, I am out twelve million dollars, and you want a finder's fee?"

"The way I see it, Condor, it don't mean a rat's ass to me what you had to pay to that spic drug dealer in Mexico.

That's your worry. I have a lot at stake myself in this money and I want my share. Comprende, mi Hermano?"

Sgt. Short could feel the room drop to subzero as the two men stared at each other. No one moved. Everyone was frozen in place as all eyes were locked on the Sheriff and El Condor. Short's mind sped through what his actions would be if things suddenly turned bloody. His chance of getting out of the room alive was zero, but he would take a few of these scumbags down with him.

"I will forget how you have just talked to me, Sheriff Perry. I will not kill you as you deserve. But know this, Señor. If you ever speak to me in this manner again, I will have you skinned alive," Gomez said in a very low, deadly voice.

The tension ratcheted back and everyone exhaled. The big man with the sandwich belched and leaned back against the wall.

"Now, let us start over. Please introduce me to this young man who you have brought into my home," Gomez said as he walked over to Short, looking him up and down.

"Old Billy here, he's my new driver and bodyguard," Perry said slapping Short on the shoulder with a big smile. "He's going to fit in just fine, helping me out with things."

"You speak very highly of him, Señor," Gomez said as he continued to walk around Sgt. Short, as if looking for flaws. "Are you a brave man, Mr. Billy? Has the Sheriff told you about me and our special relationship and how I am making him rich?"

"No, Sir, not everything, but I do know who you are and what you do," Bill said, trying to hide his fear.

"Then you know that I am a rich and a very successful businessman. I can make you wealthy beyond your simple dreams, if you are loyal to me. Is this not so?"

"Yes, Sir. I guess, if you say so."

"Oh, it is no guess, Little Billy. It is fact." Gomez stood face to face with Sgt. Short. "Will you be loyal to me, Sergeant?"

"Well, yes Sir, if that's what Sheriff Perry wants me to do."

"Sheriff Perry is one of my employees. What he wants is not important. It is what I want."

The Condor's breath was hard to take as he talked nose-to-nose with Billy.

"Yes, Sir, I can be loyal." Short's voice trembled as he spoke.

"Have you ever killed a man, Billy?"

"No, Sir, I've never been in a situation yet that required me to discharge my firearm …"

All the men broke out in loud laughter as Billy said this. Gomez stepped back in mock horror. "Madre Dias, Mother of God. I am so happy for you. I can't imagine a situation where one must *discharge his weapon.* You are a lucky policeman my friend."

After the laughter died down, the room grew quiet. Sheriff Perry had remained silent while Gomez had tested his man.

"Okay, can we get back to the business I came here for …?"

"Not yet, my fat friend. I need for Sergeant Billy to prove his loyalty to me before I see what you have brought to me," Gomez said and snapped his fingers and walked into the hallway with the entourage following on his heels.

The group followed El Condor out to a patio where a large swimming pool was lit up and fountains flowed. A man and a woman were swimming nude, splashing each other, but stopped to watch as the parade went by. Gomez held Short's elbow as they went, talking low to him.

"I want to introduce you to a man who swore his loyalty to me and then took something of great value from me. A man who swears loyalty to another and then breaks that trust is not worth much as a man is he, Mr. Billy?"

"No, Sir, I would have to agree with you on that point," Bill said, not even conscious of the words that came out of his mouth.

They entered a bungalow that sat off to the side of the walled compound and dispersed around a room that was more like a bunkhouse than a house. Short could see a hallway that ran off from the back of the large room with doors on either side, suggesting bedrooms. The de-sized room they were in had several tables and benches scattered around, along with recliners and soft informal chairs in front of a large plasma screened TV. An open kitchen at the other end of the room looked more commercial than homey, with large pots of something that smelled good bubbling away. A fat woman in an apron was busy cutting vegetables and tossing them into a cauldron on the stove. Six men were playing cards and quickly sprang up as Gomez entered the bunkhouse.

A chorus of 'Good evening, Jefe, join us for dinner Jefe, sit and play cards Jefe,' rang out as the Condor greeted them with a wave.

"Not tonight, Muchachos, there is work to be done," Gomez said as he continued through the room and down the hallway. He stopped at the last door and turned to Billy, "Now we will see if you are loyal. Inside this room is the traitor who stole something from me. He broke his oath of loyalty and can never be trusted again. I want you to go in the room and kill him. I want you to shoot him. If you do as I say, then I will know that you are loyal to me and that you will follow my orders. If you do not do as I say ... well, we will discuss that later. I give you one minute, Sergeant, to do this." Gomez opened the door and motioned Billy to go in.

Sgt. Short was shaking as he glanced at Sheriff Perry for help. Perry just looked blank and gave no sign of support. Gomez gave Billy a little shove to get him moving. Billy walked in the room letting his eyes adjust to the dim light coming from a small bathroom off to the side. He could make out a figure lying on the floor in the far corner, but couldn't pick up any details. Billy was terrified as he unsnapped his holster strap and pulled his weapon out, holding it down at his side.

"I don't want to die," a hoarse voice cried softly. "I don't want to die."

Short walked to the center of the room, pulling the hammer back on his Glock with a loud metallic click.

"Oooh, no, please no! I have a family, please don't do this. I'll give you anything, anything in the world ..."

Short raised his pistol and pointed it at the pleading form only a few feet in front of him.

"I am an agent with the DEA, they will pay you any amount of money if you save me ... just call them. I swear they'll give you anything you ask for ..."

Short swallowed acidy bile. He knew he had only a few more seconds to get this over with. '*The man said he was a*

DEA agent, maybe one of Olsen's guys, maybe he had met this guy ...' Billy thought, as he started his trigger squeeze.

The man was sobbing and kicking his legs, "Oh God, forgive me my sins …"

BAM!

Billy jumped when the pistol fired. In the flash of the muzzle he saw a man holding a hand up in anticipation of the bullet hitting him. Billy vomited and wretched.

"*Agh!* God help me," the wounded man cried out.

"He's not dead," Billy screamed in terror, raised the pistol and fired again … and again. Sobbing and screaming, he fired a fourth time. He fell to his knees and vomited until his stomach was empty. And still, he continued to retch.

The door opened and Gomez flipped the light switch on, taking in the blood and gore splattered on the far wall. "Why do you cry, Billy? This is a great day in your life. You have killed another man, and you are now my brother in blood, *mi Hermano en sangre*." Gomez said as he helped Billy to his feet. "Come, let us have a drink."

Chapter 18

Jack rolled over and threw up bile which left a coppery taste in his mouth. His forehead had the mother of all goose eggs that he could see just by looking up, and his jaw felt broken. Wherever he was, the smell of feces and something else was so strong that it made him retch. Without sitting up, he moved his head around trying to remember where he was and how he got there. Daylight was peeking through window blinds on the far wall. Something that looked like a bundle of rags or wadded blankets was piled in a corner. The wall above the blankets was smeared with large swatches of dried blood. A bathroom was off to his left. Jack pushed himself up onto his knees and then stood. Shaking and weak, he made it to the bathroom and sat on the toilet, retching again. After resting for a moment, he stood and bent over the sink and turned the one handle on full force, letting the water flow into his cupped hands. He choked on the first gulp, then sucked in water as fast as he could swallow until he was sated. As he stood looking at himself in the mirror, he was surprised at the deep reddish brown tan he had with patches of skin peeling off and the week old growth of scraggly whiskers. He smiled at himself in spite of the pain when he pulled his shirt over his head and saw the deep trucker's tan, his arms, neck, and head looked like they didn't belong to the frog-belly-white chest and back. Layers of skin were sloughing off his torso from the days of saltwater exposure, leaving a layer of new red skin in its place. But he was alive.

Jack used the shirt as a washcloth as he gave himself a quick field bath. He was tempted to strip and get in the shower, but wasn't sure who would be waiting for him when he got out. Feeling a little better, he surveyed the room. The blankets were foul with feces, old blood, and body odor. The window looked out on a tall stucco wall that had shards of glass on its top as a barrier to intruders. Anyone trying to go over the top was going to need some serious suture work … if they made it over. Jack gave the window a hard tug with no luck opening it. It had been nailed shut from the outside. At the door, he turned the knob and peeked out into a hallway. The smell of food hit him and made him faint with hunger. He closed the door quietly behind him and tiptoed down the hall. A TV was set on a cartoon channel with high squeaky voices speaking Spanish. Jack saw a group of men sitting at a table, eating and talking. One of the men spotted him and motioned him over.

"Jack, my friend, come join us. We have just started our breakfast. You must be very hungry after so long floating in the sea. And the hospital food is shit, is this not so?"

'*What the fuck*,' Jack thought as he cautiously approached the men. He didn't know if this was a trick or some ploy to get him in close, then beat him for leaving his room.

"Thank you, I am a little hungry," he said.

The man pointed to an empty chair across from him and yelled to a woman in the kitchen, "*La Tia, un Desayuno por favor*, Auntie, one more breakfast please. My friend, Jack Marsh is hungry. We need to fatten him up, make him big and strong before we start our day," the big man said with a huge grin on his face.

The smile reminded Jack of the serial killer years back who dressed like a clown to entertain little boys before he killed them and buried them in shallow graves under his house. The man's hair was slick with oil and pulled back into a ponytail. His brows looked like one big caterpillar which ran all the way across his forehead, and his beady eyes were lifeless, like a vulture's waiting for its meal to die. His host had an unbuttoned, flowery shirt that exposed a black hairy chest and several heavy gold chains with religious medallions, charms, even a Buddha dangling from one. But the one thing that held Jack's attention was the long scar that ran at an angle across and down his stomach. Whoever sewed this guy up didn't know what he was doing it was jagged and nasty, and looked like it had hurt like hell.

"You like my scar?" the man asked, puffing his stomach out. "When I was a young man working in the cane fields in Cuba, a man came to me and said that I had fucked his woman. I told him I had not touched his woman. I did not even know who she was. He was crazy with jealousy and swung his machete at me cutting me open as you see." Gomez ran his hand along the scar line to demonstrate the cut. "I remember seeing my insides coming out and screaming. The man ran off into the cane field to hide. The woman who brought our lunches every day to the field knew of these matters and pushed everything back inside and began sewing me up with a piece of string from her apron and a needle used for lancing blisters on the workers' hands. As you can see, it is not a pretty scar, but the woman saved my life that day. I lost many days' work because of the cut, but soon I was better. Meanwhile, the man who cut me had been promoted to the mill that crushes the cane and takes out the sugar. One day when he was the only one inside the mill, he *accidently* fell into the crusher and was cut into very small pieces, crushed along with the cane, and then passed through the dryer that makes the sugar hard. No one knows how it was possible that he fell into the crusher, since the mouth of the machine was over ten feet above the floor and no man would have a reason to be there." Gomez smiled. "What do you think of my story, Jack?"

"I think I will never eat brown sugar again," Jack said.

"Ha-ha, very good answer, Jack. I agree, maybe I will not eat brown sugar either." Gomez's smile faded. "Jack, maybe we should have our talk now. I think it is time we discussed our problem, what do you think?"

"I'm not sure what problem you are referring to, I'm not even sure where I am or how I got here. The last thing I remember is Sheriff Perry and Sgt. Short shaking me down for weapons."

"Yes, Sheriff Perry told me all about that. It was he who brought you to me and said that you have my ten million dollars. Did the Sheriff tell the truth, Jack, do you have my ten million dollars? Sometimes I don't know what to believe from that man."

Jack's heart picked up a few beats when he realized that the man in front of him was indeed El Condor — Gomez — reportedly one of the most ruthless criminals to ever cross over from Cuba.

"Mr. Gomez, I know you won't believe this, but I don't have your money. I mean, I did at one time, but now it's gone," Jack said as he tried to think how much he could say and remain alive.

"Jack, I am a very patient man in these matter. One reasonable man talking to another. Today is such a beautiful day and I am in such a good mood. I want us to be friends, but I will tell you that I can go from nice to very nasty with a snap of my fingers. So how should we proceed?"

"Well, I certainly want to help you out, Mr. Gomez, but the truth is that the money is on the bottom of the Florida Strait, bolted down to the deck of the *Island Girl*, which sank during the storm."

"So the money is on the bottom of the sea and is wet and ruined?"

"No sir, it's not ruined. It's inside a watertight container. But you are correct. It is on the bottom of the sea, so it's basically gone," Jack said, feeling that it would be safer if he just leveled with the Condor and tried to get out of this alive.

"So you stole my money, put it on your boat, then the boat sank, it is on the bottom of the ocean, and I am now a poor man with no money. Is this a good summary, Jack?"

"Well, close. I was hiding the money until I could find out who owned it. Then Don Cona, one of your competitors, said it was his money, and a DEA agent named Olsen was trying to get it, so I hid it inside the chamber on the boat until I was sure whose it was. If I had known it was yours, I would have returned it right away ..."

"*You fucking liar*," Gomez yelled and slapped Jack in the face, knocking him out of his chair and on to the floor. "You think I believe all this bullshit? Sheriff Perry told me that it was you who killed the bum in the cemetery after you tortured him to tell you where the money was hidden. Your friend, the Sheriff, then told me that you killed Olsen and the black man to shut them up about your involvement. I tell you this, Jack, Agent Olsen worked for me for a long time as a loyal employee. So when I heard that he was dead, it was as if a knife had been stuck in my back. When I heard of his murder, I swore that I would avenge him. Last night, it was Sheriff Perry who told me it was you who had killed Olsen, and that you have been working with Don Cona all along to take my money to Cuba and hide it there with his friends. You think I don't know what that old thief is up to? I know all about his plan to kill Fidel and put his man in power," Gomez yelled in a frenzy, blowing spit all over Jack as he screamed and cursed. "I know about the men who were sent to Cuba to kill Castro. Who do you think warned El Presidente about the planned assassination? Who do you think has sent hit men to kill this peasant calling himself the Don of Havana?" he continued in a rage, kicking Jack as he yelled.

Jack rolled with the kicks, using his hands and arms to cover his head as he took the body blows and tried to roll up into a ball as tight as he could. Finally, Gomez ran out of steam and flopped down in his chair, breathing hard.

"Jack, you know that I am going to kill you, don't you?" Gomez said, once he had his breathing under control. "I am a very rich man, Jack. Ten million dollars is not so much money to me. In my business I can make that much in just a few days' time. I have so much money that I have trouble just trying to hide it." Gomez stomped the floor loudly with his boot. "Would you believe, that just below this floor is a room packed so tight with money that a mouse cannot get inside? I have a warehouse that is also packed with money that I cannot get rid of, so for me to lose ten million dollars is nothing. The problem, Jack, is simple. I must kill you for stealing my money, because if I don't, my business competitors would see it as a sign of weakness on my part. Then what do you think would happen? I will tell you. They would come at me like the piranhas and eat at me until there is nothing left, not even my bones. But, if I kill you and the people around you, then they will see that El Condor is still the Jefe Grande. Do you see my reasoning, Jack?"

Jack had stretched out trying to work the pain out of his body from the kicks. One especially hard kick had hit him on the tailbone, and it was shooting jolts of electricity up his spine, like fuses blowing.

"Gomez, I don't want to die, but I'm not afraid of it. I just hate to die for some stupid fucking reason. I stumbled into this pig-fuck by accident and thought I could make a few bucks out of it. I was wrong. So I was caught. But is it worth being killed over? Hell, no! If I had the money, I would return it, and that's the truth," Jack said, sitting up.

Gomez laughed loudly, rocking back and forth in his chair, "Jack, I like you, you have cajones. Most men beg when they are told they are going to die. It is too bad you are not a crook like me." Gomez kicked back in his chair, smiling and scratching his morning whiskers. "I tell you what I will do for you, my brave friend. After our talk this morning, I was going to have my brothers here beat you to death and deposit your body in your bar in Key West. This way all my competition would see that the Condor is still flying high. Then, just to make sure that they still respected and feared me, I was going to kill your partner, Thomas Hicks, and his new "son" Miguel ..."

"*Tommy! Mike!* No way, they didn't have anything to do with this! You're crazy Gomez, why kill innocent people ...?"

"*Silence*! I demand silence. I will kill you this very minute if you dare to interrupt me again," Gomez screamed, standing up cursing in Spanish as he flipped open a long bladed knife and threw it at Jack. Before Jack could react to the blade coming at him, it stuck three inches away from his ear, quivering. Jack just stared at the knife as Gomez leaned down and pulled the blade out of the wooden floor.

"Please do not think that I missed. My knife went exactly where I wanted it to go, Señor Big Mouth. Next time it will sink deep into your heart," Gomez said as he folded the knife, put back in his hip pocket, and gave another kick to Jack's side. "Get up, I need to talk, and you need to listen."

Jack sat across from the Condor as the other men gathered back around the table and took their seats.

"Jack, are you a gambling man? I think so. I think this because of the gamble you took to steal my money. I am bored and need some excitement in my life. All work and no play is bad for one's health. So I have an idea. I am going to give your friend the chance to live. I am going to give you the chance to return my money to me. If you return it, I will not kill Señor Hicks or the boy. If you do not return it, then you will watch as I kill them."

"You're asking the impossible, Gomez. I can't return the money. I told you it is on the bottom of the Florida Strait, bolted down to the deck of the *Island Girl*."

"Oh, I think you are a very clever man and know where the boat sank. At least I hope you are that clever. Otherwise, I am sorry, but I will just have to kill those two innocent people, and then kill you, of course. Since I won't need you and I have a reputation to keep, the sooner I finish this business up the better."

Gomez snapped his fingers and tapped his coffee cup for a refill. The Señora hustled over and filled all the cups.

"What you say next is very important, Jack, so take your time answering. Can you find the location of where the boat sank? If you think you can, then I will make all the arrangements for us to go find it and retrieve it. If you do this, then I swear to you that your friends will live."

Jack's mind was spinning like a dervish as he tried to make sense of what Gomez was saying. The man was so irrational and psychotic that at any moment he could snap and kill without any hesitation. If he found the money, then Tommy and little Mikey would live, but he himself was still doomed. As for trusting Gomez, he didn't. He needed time to plan an escape and get out of the Keys with Tommy and the kid. He knew the approximate location of where the *Island Girl* went down and it was marginal whether she lay on the shelf at a hundred feet down or had slipped over the side and was now so far down that special diving equipment would be needed to reach her. The chances that the sonar beacon on the life jacket he had activated during the storm was still pinging out a pulse were slim to none. The battery life was only forty-eight hours and it's been down there now for at least six days. Jack needed time. He knew what he had to tell Gomez, even though he knew his fate was sealed unless a miracle happened.

"Yes, I can find her. With the right equipment, and given enough time, I can bring the chamber up. I can't make any commitments about the Cuban Navy or the Coasties poking around watching to see what we are after, but my part will be straightforward," Jack said.

"Excellent," Gomez said, as he massaged his palms as if washing away a problem. "Tell me what you need and I will see that you have it. I will spare no expense. We will have the best of everything. Jack, you have made me very happy. We are going treasure hunting just like in the movies. I will be the Captain in charge of order and discipline, and you will be my first mate who dies at the end of the story, ha-ha," Gomez laughed loudly while the men around the table laughed even louder out of respect and fear of the Condor.

Jack even managed a sickly smile, but down deep he was seething at the audacity of this mutt to assume that he would go quietly to his death. The first chance he got, he was going to take this fat man out.

Chapter 19

Captain Price kicked the cafeteria door open out of frustration as he and Lt. Mathers entered the packed facility. It was change of shift at Jackson Memorial Hospital and the place was crowded with nurses, doctors, patients' relatives, and members of half a dozen law agencies sitting around shooting the breeze. It had been a long night for Captain Price. He hadn't had any sleep for over thirty hours and he was fatigued. The shock and disappointment of Marsh skipping out on him after arranging a safe haven for him and his friends in a small hospital in Boca where they could recover in safety, was blown. Within minutes of Price finding Marsh gone, the word had flashed up and down the hallway and pandemonium broke out. There were so many conflicting stories that no one fully understood what had happened. The TV reporters went live, announcing the mysterious disappearance of the John Doe who had been recovering from his days at sea. Another reported that the man was Jack Marsh, an accused murderer from Key West. A third even said that Marsh had been murdered in his sleep to keep him quiet about a cartel drug heist that had gone bad.

As the next few hours flashed by, Lt. Mathers had joined with Price to try and pick up Marsh's trail. Reports that Sheriff Perry had been seen at about the same time Marsh disappeared alarmed both lawmen. Lt. Mathers tried calling Sgt. Short's cell and left a message to call back. That was four hours ago and still not a word. Mathers was worried that Short might be in trouble if Sheriff Perry suspected Short of deception or of reporting on his activities. Mathers had also notified the other members of the task force to call him if and when they saw the Sheriff or Short. The Lieutenant had a bad feeling that things were coming to a head, but he didn't know where to start. At some point, most of the lawmen gave up their posts at the V.A. and set up station across the street at Jackson Memorial. Captain Price had pulled rank and got him and Mathers in the room where Tommy Hicks was. Both men were surprised when they entered the room and found a woman and a young man sitting bedside talking with Hicks.

"Who are you two people?" Price demanded. "This man is not supposed to have any visitors."

"I might ask you the same question," Coco said, standing up and facing off with the two men. "I must ask that you leave the room immediately. My friend is not well and needs rest."

Lt. Mathers touched Price's elbow. "It's okay, Captain, this is Jack Marsh's partner at the Sand Bar, Ms. Coco Duvalier. She can probably help us fill in the blanks about tonight."

"Lt. Mathers, excuse me, I didn't recognize you out of uniform. What's the latest on Jack? Any news on where he is? We have been out of our minds with worry," Coco said.

"As of now, you probably know more than we do. I should probably ask you why you're here or how is it that you even knew to come here," Mathers said.

"Jack called me around eight last night, and said that he had just checked himself out of the V.A. and asked me to meet him at 11:00 p.m. at the Four Seasons Hotel on Bay Front. He sounded scared and said that people were after him and not to be late. I was so relieved to know that he was alive that I told him that I would meet him, no matter what. I was scared because I didn't know what was going on, so I called Lamont and asked that he come with me," Coco said rapidly. "We arrived at the Four Seasons at a quarter 'til eleven and waited until two. Jack never showed. Jack had told me that Tommy was in Jackson, so after giving up waiting for Jack, we came over here." She shrugged her shoulders as she finished up.

"That fits in with the basic time line," Price said to Mathers softly, with his back to the others in the room. "We don't know any more than we did ten minutes ago other than Perry must have grabbed Marsh and is holding him somewhere on the murder charges."

"Captain, if the Sheriff had Marsh, he would have been back in Key West hours ago. And, as of twenty minutes ago, he still hasn't reported in."

Price thought for a few moments, "Ms. Duvalier, who are the other two people who came in with Mr. Hicks and Mr. Marsh ..."

"I can answer that," Tommy said trying to sit up. "The boy is my ... son, Michael. He is spending time with me while his mother is ... uh, busy up on the mainland."

"Your son? Hicks, I didn't even know you had ever been married before, much less have a son," Mathers said.

"Well, how would you have known, Lieutenant? It's not as if we're running buddies or anything. I keep my personal life pretty much to myself. His mother is Cuban. We've been divorced for a long time and she has custody," Tommy lied.

"OK, I can go with that for now. So who's the other guy who came in with you?"

"Uh, which other guy, Lieutenant?" Tommy said, scratching his head, trying to remember.

"The guy with all the black curly hair and the gut shot."

"Oh, that guy. That's Jack's friend from the bar, Junior something or other."

"Yeah? Junior, as in Tony Cona's bodyguard, Junior?" Mathers asked.

"I guess. I don't know anything about all that. Jack just said he was coming along for the ride."

"What was this ride all about? How was it that two of you were shot, a son suddenly appears, the *Island Girl* drops off the radar, and then you guys float in life preservers for well over a hundred miles north of where you told the Coast Guard you would be before the strongest hurricane of the season hit?" Mathers asked.

"Damn, Lieutenant, that is exactly right on all counts. We were out on the blue to test the new stabilizers on the boat. When the storm hit, we were blown off course into Cuban waters and attacked by the Cuban Navy. They shot up the boat, shot Junior and me, and the *Girl* sank out from under us. Dirty bastards. That is exactly what happened, and that's exactly what I'm telling the insurance company, too."

Captain Price was impressed with Tommy's half-truth and half-lie by leaving out the covert Special Ops team's involvement and how the *Island Girl* had been tricked into helping the State Department's scheme to assassinate Castro and replace him with someone who would toe the pro-democracy line while the old time Mafioso set up operations again. Price was convinced that Hicks and Marsh were just tools in the bigger picture of international diplomacy and trickery. Just a couple of guys seeing the chance to pick up some free money and fell in way over their heads. His thought was that he needed to get Hicks and the kid out of this hospital and away from anyone trying to shut them up about the Spec Op fiasco. As for Junior, he was on his own. Don Cona could worry about what happened to him.

"Mr. Hicks, I'll level with you. At this time, we are not sure if Marsh is alive or dead. Hell, we're not even sure where he is. I need to assume that your life is in danger as well, since you both were involved in the … uh, shall we say, clandestine activities off the coast of Cuba. I happen to know that several different government agencies are upset with the way that turned out and they are looking for someone to … uh, hold accountable. Then, there is the situation with Sheriff Perry's involvement. We suspect that he is trying to settle a vendetta between Marsh, Don Cona, and himself regarding a missing ten million dollars." Price paused for a moment. "You don't happen to know where the missing money is, do you, Hicks?"

"I don't have any idea what you are talking about, Captain. I don't know anything about any clandestine activities off Cuba and I sure don't know where ten million dollars is," Tommy said. "And as for Jack being alive or dead, I know Jack better than anyone and the only way he would be dead is if someone snuck up on him from behind and shot him. Otherwise, he is one of the toughest men I know, so don't be too quick to count him out. Marsh will be around long after the rest of us have hung it up."

Chapter 20

Jack was sitting on the floor, leaning back against the wall, watching the closed door across from him. After the morning's breakfast ass-kicking, Jack was escorted back to his room and told to get cleaned up, and that fresh clothes would be given to him. Back in the room, he had stripped down and given himself a good exam, top to bottom. Everything checked out, except the skin between his toes was gone and left raw and burning, plus two toes had lost their nails. Other than that, he was still sunburned and covered in peeling, blistered skin where it had been exposed, but was healing nicely. As he stood checking himself, the Señora came in with an arm load of towels and clean clothes and started jabbering in Spanish as she gave him an appreciative wink. Jack mimed shaving and the Señorita laughed and hurried off, coming back in less than a minute with a razor and shaving cream and placed them on the sink. She swatted Jack on his bare butt as she left the room.

A couple of hours had gone by. Jack had dropped off into a dream-filled sleep where he was back on the water floating up and down. Big Miguel was calling to him from far off ...

"Jack, get up, we have much to do before we leave," one of Gomez's men said as he gave Jack an easy kick to wake him.

"Yeah, I'm awake."

"Good, my name is Ortiz. You and I will become good friends over the next few days. We are diving buddies and will be the ones who go down in search of the Condor's treasure. Follow me, we must see to our gear before we leave," Ortiz said, as if they had been buddies forever.

Jack followed Ortiz across the lawn to the dock where a huge pleasure yacht was tied off. Jack recognized the boat as one of the latest luxury designs from Italy with all the latest state-of-the-art electronics and navigational gear sticking up from the bridge, three decks up. The second deck appeared to be the owner's deck or party deck and then the main deck salon and gathering areas.

"Ortiz, does this belong to Gomez?" Jack asked looking at the sleek lines and all the bright work.

"Isn't she beautiful? Her name is *Malagueña Salerosa* after the beautiful romantic Spanish song. Señor Gomez spends all of his time on her when he is not busy in Miami. Sometimes we just cruise around the islands in the Caribbean, dropping anchor for a few days in secluded spots, so the Señor and his guests can swim and relax."

"I assume you work for Gomez, right?" Jack asked.

"Oh sure, I have worked on the Señor's boats for several years. I am rated as second mate and, when I am not working directly under Capitán Juarez, then I am responsible for the Señor's guests when they are in the water," Ortiz volunteered. "In Cuba I attended the Academia Naval and then for four years I was Teniente de Fragata, a junior lieutenant," he said snapping to attention and saluting Marsh.

Jack laughed along with Ortiz. He liked his relaxed manner and openness and just couldn't see Ortiz fitting in with the other thugs working for Gomez.

"Well, Lieutenant, I was only a corporal in the Marines so I guess you outrank me. What do you want me to do, besides chip paint?"

"I think once we have all of our diving needs sorted out, the Capitán will notify the Señor that we are ready. But first we must go over the charts with Capitán Juarez, so he knows where we are going."

"Let's get started. The sooner we get this over with the better … I guess," Jack said with a little twinge of fear deep inside.

"Jack, look it is none of my business what the trouble is between you and the Señor, so do not feel that you need to share with me. I just want you to know that my job is on the boat. Whatever it is the Jefe does is his business, I keep my nose out of it, and when I hear things and see things I look the other way. I think I like you and I will work with you honestly and as a fellow military comrade, but if trouble comes, I must not be seen as being involved. I am sorry, Jack, but I must think of my family first," Ortiz said.

"I understand. I promise I won't get you into any trouble, but if you see me doing anything unusual or something that is not an ordinary diving procedure, then I would ask that you just look the other way. Will you do that for me?"

"Yes, I will do this. In Cuba we have a saying, 'A dog is the best friend to have. It sees everything, but it knows nothing.' Now, let's get to work," Ortiz said, clapping Jack on the back.

An hour and a half later Jack and Ortiz had gone over all the diving gear, checking tanks, regulators, B.C. vests (Buoyancy Compensator), masks, fins, tools, everything they would need, if and when they found the *Island Girl*. Working underwater required that they have a dive plan that included bottom time, depth, dives per day, emergency procedures, and communications. Once the two men had laid out their plans, they reported to Capitán Juarez to share them with him and to work out the course to the general site and then establish a grid search for the lost boat.

"So, we do not have an exact location for this sunken craft, Señor Marsh?" Capitán Juarez asked as the three men hunched over the chart for the Florida Strait and waters off of north Cuba.

"I'm sorry, Captain, but we were in the hurricane when she went down and all of our electronics were out. My last known location when we were in the eye of the storm was just southeast of the Cay Sal bank," Jack said picking up a set of calipers. "We came out of Santa Cruz del Norte on a north east heading. By that time the storm had backtracked and was moving west, so my plan was to run east until we cleared it. We were fighting the storm and the current when the Cuban Navy found us and opened fire. At that point I knew we were north northeast of Cardenas. I ducked into a wall of water and lost the frigate, then an hour later, I popped out inside the eye. By then the boat was pretty well shot up and taking on water, but one engine was still running and I headed us back into the northeast side of the storm's wall," Jack said as he walked the calipers up the chart. "I'm not sure how long it was from that point until we abandoned ship, but I guess we were carried at least another twenty miles by the rotation of the storm, which would have put us around this location," Jack said, pinning the calipers to a tiny spot off the Cay Sal Bank called Muertos Cay.

Lieutenant Ortiz and Captain Juarez examined the chart closely for a few minutes, discussing their options.

"Mr. Marsh, are you familiar with the Cay Sal Bank?" Juarez asked tapping the chart.

"No sir, I'm not. I just know where it is."

"Cay Sal has the reputation for being the most bombed spot on earth. The U.S. and Cuba have used the spot for naval and bombing exercises for decades. There are tons of unexploded bombs and shells on the Bank and surrounding waters that make it extremely dangerous for anyone to venture onto the Cay. My advice would be to forget whatever is down there and to stay away from the area."

Jack knew the stakes for his surviving had just gone up again. If the Captain convinced El Condor that it was too risky to go there, then there was no need to keep Jack alive, along with Tommy and Mikey. Then, if Gomez did decide to take the risk, Jack would be in danger working around any unexploded bombs or munitions lying around the work site. He was screwed any way he looked at it.

"What advice are you speaking of, Capitán?" Gomez asked as he entered the wheelhouse. "I was just coming aboard to see what is taking so long. My guests and I have been waiting far too long for such a simple trip to be organized."

"I apologize, Señor Gomez. We were discussing the location where Señor Marsh thinks the sunken vessel is. I must report that I do not recommend that we enter this particular area because of the danger to you and the *Malagueña*.

"Oh, what is the danger?" Gomez perked up at the mention of any potential harm to himself.

"Señor, the area is a closed military bombing range, and I am afraid that some unexploded munitions might be triggered accidently by the divers as they work, or just explode on their own."

"So the danger is to the divers and not to me or the boat is that correct?" Gomez asked.

"Well, Señor, if we are anchored above the work site, then we would be in danger, *verdad,* true?"

Like lightning, Gomez's hand shot out in a blur and slapped Juarez across the face. "You imbecile! Even a child would know to anchor away from the work site and let the divers swim or take the Zodiac rubber boat to the dive site. If you cannot figure out something this simple without me to help you think then what am I doing trusting my beautiful boat to you?" Gomez screamed in rage. "Now get us ready to leave in thirty minutes without any more stupid concerns," he said and stomped out of the wheelhouse.

Juarez regained his composure, straightening his braided Capitán's hat as he looked off into space.

"Prepare the ship for departure, Teniente," he said with dignity. We cast lines off as soon as the owner is aboard."

"Si, mi Capitán."

Chapter 21

An hour later, the *Malagueña Salerosa* had cleared the channel markers leading out of Biscayne Bay and had entered the northern reaches of the Florida Strait, motoring at a smooth twenty knots. The foamy green wake the big yacht's propellers kicked up ran a straight line due north as Capitán Juarez held her nose running due south. The route would take them steady on this southerly course for five hours and then cut south by southeast out over the Bahamas trench where they would loiter overnight. At daybreak, Capitán Juarez would change the heading back to the southwest and approach the Cay Sal Bank in daylight, rather than dark. Even with all the electronic equipment on board, he still thought that the human eye could pick out danger better than any fancy Japanese gear.

Jack was given the very bottom bunk on a stack of four that were built into the bulkhead. Each bunk had a curtain that could be pulled closed for privacy, but beyond that, everything else was communal. There were six crew members including the Capitán. Ortiz had a top bunk on the other side of the space that was a little larger than what the other seaman had. A cook, a waiter, an engineer, and a deck hand each had a bunk in the space. Capitán Juarez slept forward somewhere in his own cabin. Before Gomez and his party arrived, Jack was told to go below and stay in the crew's quarters and not to leave the room by himself. Someone would come for him later if he was needed.

Jack stretched out in his bunk and pulled the curtain closed. The vibration from the powerful motors through the hull was comforting and he drifted off into a peaceful sleep. The smell of food pulled him awake. He glanced at the luminous dial on his wristwatch and saw that he had been asleep for over five hours, the longest he had slept in days. Feeling refreshed, he pulled his curtain back, rolled out on the deck, and stood. The suddenness of his moves startled two men who were eating at the common table.

"*Madre Dias*, Mother of God," one of the men yipped in surprise.

His companion laughed once he realized that they were not in danger. "It is only the *Yanqui*. Iyeee, you gave us the scare, Señor," he said, embarrassed.

"Sorry about that," Jack said, stretching as he worked the kinks out of his body. "What's to eat? I'm starved."

"Come and join us. We have fish, beans, rice, and the plantains," the older of the two offered.

Jack sat as the younger man pulled a plate and silverware out of a cabinet and placed it in front of Jack. Without any preamble, Jack dove in. The food was delicious and plentiful. The only sounds coming from the three men were grunts and groans of appreciation as they ate in silence. Finally, the older man sat back, belched loudly, and stuck a toothpick in the corner of his mouth.

Comment [CC]:

"So, Señor, is it true that you stole El Condor's money and now we are going to get it back from the bottom of the ocean?"

Jack finished off his coffee and sat back relaxed. "Well, it's partly true about the money. I didn't actually steal it myself, but I did end up with it. However, Mr. Gomez thinks I was the one who took it. Actually, that money bounced around so much I can't even remember who actually took it from Gomez."

"It is whispered that once he gets his money back, Señor Gomez is going to kill you. Is this true?"

"Yeah, I think that's his plan. But we don't have the money back yet, so for this minute I am still hopeful ..."

The cabin door swung open and one of Gomez's mutts filled the opening.

"Marsh, come with me," he demanded.

"… Spoke too soon," Jack said, as he got up to leave. His two dinner partners crossed themselves as he closed the door behind him.

Jack followed the big man up two decks and entered the main deck salon where a party was underway. Salsa music was playing loudly as two women gyrated to the beat. Several men sat around, drinks in hand, as a white-jacketed waiter balanced a tray and worked his way around the large cabin.

"Jack." Gomez called out when he spotted Jack entering the room. "Everyone, listen to me, listen," Gomez said drunkenly, as he threw an arm over Jack's shoulder, pulling him in tight. "This is our guest of honor. This is Jack Marsh, the man who stole my money, but has agreed to give it back. He has even offered to dive down to retrieve it from the bottom of the ocean where he hid it from me. Ah, but the Condor knows all and sees all. No one can hide anything from me," he said as he tapped the corner of his eye.

All the guests dutifully laughed and applauded as their master continued to hug Jack, more for stability than bonhomie fellowship. The attention was soon off Jack as he helped Gomez lower himself into a comfortable chair. The waiter came by and handed Gomez a fresh drink, dark with aged whiskey.

"Jack, I like you," Gomez slurred, and motioned for him to sit down by him. "I do not want to kill you, you understand that don't you? But you have put me in such a terrible position with all my enemies that I must kill you. If I let you live, then I am committing suicide. The Jamaicans are the worst. They will come for me with voodoo spells and their jujus and then slice me up with their knives as soon as I am asleep."

"Hire more men to protect you," Jack said, only half listening as his eyes locked on to Bill Short's as Short entered the Salon with a woman hugging his waist, and Sheriff Perry right behind him with another woman.

Gomez spotted them as they came forward. "Sgt. Short, come here, I want you to meet someone."

Jack stood up as the two lawmen answered the Condor's bidding.

"We've met," Jack said, staring hard at Billy.

"Hi, Jack, sorry we have to meet like this, but things have changed. I'm with Señor Gomez now. It was just too hard to make it where I want to go on a deputy's pay," Short said as the two men stared at each other.

"Ah, two friends, reunited through the grace of God … *and El Condor*," Gomez laughed. "Armando, bring my guests drinks," Gomez snapped his fingers. "We will have a toast. "Everybody listen to me, listen," Gomez demanded as he stood weaving. "A toast to the victim and the victor … *Salute*." A chorus of '*Salute*' rang out as the crowd threw back their drinks, all except Jack and Bill. They both stood looking at Gomez, puzzled.

"Señor Gomez, excuse me, but what is it that you toasted? 'The *victim, and the victor*?' What do you mean?"

"Ha-ha, Billy. I was with you when you made your bones. Now you are going to make bones again, but this time for my friends to watch. Hahaha," El Condor said drunkenly. "Tomorrow, after we have my money safely aboard the *Malagueña*, you will kill Mr. Jack Marsh. We will take videos so I can send copies to all the Putá Jamaicans."

Billy snapped his head back to look at Jack. "I can't do that. Jack is my friend. I won't do it."

Jack stood his ground as the room became deathly quiet. The only sound came from the salsa music still blaring. The dancing girls stood frozen in mid-step.

"Excuse me," Gomez said, so softly it was almost a whisper, his eyes went unfocused for a moment and his face slack.

"You heard me, I draw the line. Jack is a friend of mine, I can't shoot him, and I won't," Billy said, standing his ground and still staring at Jack.

Without warning, Gomez palmed his drink glass and smashed it, edge on, into Billy's face breaking the glass on his teeth and nose. A shard slivered off and jammed into his right eye, shattering the retina into a thousand tiny frosted puzzle shapes. As Billy grabbed his bleeding face, Gomez kicked him in the crotch doubling him over. Billy went down on his knees, forehead on the ground, crying out in pain. Gomez snapped his fingers and one of his flunkies handed him a large revolver.

"Nobody ever talks to me that way. If I say you do something, you do it," he said, as he cocked the hammer, placed the muzzle on the crown of Billy's head, and fired.

KA-BAM!

The boom in the close quarters was like a cannon shot going off. Blood sprayed out behind Billy, splattering across Sheriff Perry's trousers and boots as he jumped back.

"Shit, look at this, would ya?" Perry said as he surveyed the splatter, wiping one boot at a time on the back of his pant leg.

Jack stood in shock. Everything had happened so fast he hadn't had a chance to react. The only thing he could focus on was the boots Perry was wearing. They were the same pair Pointman had taken off the dead man. Seemed like years ago.

"And you, Marsh. I swear to the Virgin Mother that if I didn't need you, I would kill you right now. Get out of my sight … and take this piece of shit with you," he said as he kicked Billy.

Jack went over to the wet bar and grabbed several bar towels, placing them around Billy's head. Then he picked Billy up in his arms and left by the side hatchway. Out on deck, the salty air had never smelled or felt so good as Jack headed for the back of the boat. Once he was on the aft deck, he put Billy's body down gently and sat next to it. Jack still wasn't over the surprise of seeing Billy with Sheriff Perry on the boat. He knew that Perry was rumored to be dirty, but Billy was his friend and would never go rogue like this. Something else was going on that he didn't know about. There were so many people involved in this whole crazy pig fuck... Special Ops troopers, some crazy assed CIA type, Don Cona and the Mafia, the money, Olsen and Ike, probably dead, based on Gomez's comment earlier that day. Captain Price from the Florida Bureau of Investigation, Gomez himself, filthy rich but willing to risk everything to retrieve his missing ten million dollars. Tommy and Mikey's lives at risk, and then his own life in the hands of a terribly sick psychopath. Jack wasn't sure there was a way out of this fix. The only thing that even stood a chance was for him to kill everyone on the boat and escape on the zodiac, but the chance of him doing that were so slim it wasn't even worth thinking about. If he could get to the radio and send a message or send out a distress signal to the Coast Guard, maybe they would send a cutter out to investigate.

"Jack, here let us help you," Ortiz said, as he and the two crew members he had had dinner with squatted down and lifted Billy's body.

"Wait, let me take his personal stuff out of his pockets. There might be something there to send to his family," Jack said as he took Billy's wallet, keys, a few coins and put it all in his pocket.

Without a word, the four men picked Bill Short's body up, carried it out to the dive platform, and let it slip into the prop wash. Within seconds Billy was gone. The three Cubans crossed themselves, kissing their fingers in supplication as Jack wiped tears from his eyes.

Jack was wide awake, tossing and turning in his bunk. Finally, he had enough and rolled out, making his way over to the small kitchen sink area where the crew brewed coffee and stuffed the cabinets with junk food and munchies. Jack stuck his mouth under the faucet and gulped the chlorine tasting water, then splashed his face and neck. As he reached for a dishtowel, he caught site of a cell phone sitting at the end of the counter, its red blinking light giving notice that it was up and running. Jack took a quick look around the cabin, saw that the bunk curtains were all pulled shut, and snatched the phone up. A shot of straight adrenaline hit his stomach as he eased out the cabin door and made for the back work deck. Outside, in the fresh sea air, a billion stars lit up the night. A quick look around and he flipped open the phone and dialed Coco's number from memory.

After an eternity of four rings, Coco's voice kicked in telling the caller to leave a message, "It's me. I'm in big trouble and need help. I'm on Gomez's boat and will be at Cay Sal Bank at daylight. Once I retrieve the chamber with Gomez's money in it, he plans to kill me. Billy Short is dead, killed by Gomez. Sheriff Perry is on board as a friendly guest, total guests around six men, four women. The men are armed. The crew is not a threat. Hurry."

Jack flipped the phone closed, took a couple of deep breaths of fresh air and worked his way back to the cabin. Closing the door silently behind, he put the cell phone back where he found it, and slipped into his bunk. Across the cabin, Ortiz smiled as he pulled his blanket up tight around his neck against the air conditioner blowing just outside his bunk.

Chapter 22

The *Malagueña Salerosa* came around to the east side of Cay Sal from the southern approach at five knots, barely making headway. An old Cuban fishing trawler had pulled away from the area as Captain Juarez worked his way up the Cay. The Cay was actually a reef that ran a mile long and a half mile wide with only a few square meters of coral rising above the surface, serving as a nesting and rest area for hundreds of seabirds. The water depth was one to three feet across the reef during low tide and totally submerged at high tide. Tropical sea life was abundant on and around the Cay as it sloped from a few feet deep down to a hundred and fifty, then quickly dropped off to four and five hundred feet. SCUBA divers had nicknamed the Cay the Wedding Cake Key years before because of the resemblance to a multi-tiered cake, shelving off at each consecutive layer.

Jack was on the bridge with Ortiz and Capitán Juarez watching the sonar scope scanning the bottom for the *Island Girl*. The real-time view of the bottom gave them a clear shot of what they were motoring over. Coral heads, rubble, an occasional bomb casing, junk that had escaped the Gulf Stream off to the west and eventually found its way to the Cay, all now lay on the bottom. Jack had asked Juarez to turn the volume up on the sound receiver in the off-chance that the life vest safety unit was still pinging. The sound that came over the hydrophone was filled with hundreds of little chirps, peeps, and clicks as the millions of tropical sea creatures went about their morning business, but no manmade pings bounced back. Jack kept a sharp eye out on the horizon, hoping to see someone coming to his rescue. At one point, Ortiz and Jack caught each other scanning the horizon and quickly looked away. Capitán Juarez was sharply dressed in his white summer uniform and hadn't mentioned last night's murder or the dumping of Bill Short's body overboard. It was like he was in total denial of his true circumstances and that his master was a murderer.

By 09:00 Gomez and his guests were in full party mode with salsa music blaring from every speaker on the ship and laughter and loud talking coming from the salon deck. Two of the women were sunbathing topless on the forward bow, perfecting their tans as Sheriff Perry, with just his trousers and boots on, ogled them from a few feet away. Ortiz jabbed Jack with an elbow and nodded at Perry, "If he doesn't put a shirt on soon he will be in much pain in a few hours."

Jack smirked, "Let the fucker fry."

Gomez came onto the bridge looking pale and hung over. He was dressed in linen walking shorts and a bright colored shirt with a parrot print, unbuttoned, displaying his gold bling, "Why haven't we located the boat yet, Marsh? We have been running back and forth across this same area since sunup."

"It takes time. We're running a grid pattern over the area where the *Island Girl* went down. With the water this clear and all the electronics on board your boat we'll find her if she's down there," Jack said as he kept his eyes on the screen.

"What do you mean, *if* she's down there? You told me that you knew where she was."

"Just give us time. We're doing everything we can to find her. We're tracking between 100 and 150 feet down now. Unless she slipped over the side and went deeper, we should see her on this pass," Jack said.

"Do you agree with Marsh, Ortiz?"

"Yes, Señor. I think, based on all the data, we should find her soon," Ortiz said confidently.

"Notify me the minute you spot something," Gomez said and left the bridge, wiping his face with a large bandana kerchief.

As the *Malagueña* skirted a small hump of coral known as Dos Muertos Cay, something caught Ortiz's eye on the scope.

"Jack, look," he said pointing to an object that didn't fit with the rest of the area below.

Jack peered closely and said, "Captain, back off your motors. I think we've found her."

All three men bent close trying to determine what they were looking at. Eighty feet below was a manmade object lying on a steep incline of loose rubble and coral. Whatever it was, it appeared to have slipped off one of the cake layers and slid part way down to the next layer before it caught up on something. Ortiz fine-tuned the focus and a boat hull came in to sharp view. It was the *Island Girl* with her bow pointing almost straight up, as if she were mounted on a gantry waiting to be launched back to the surface. Jack wasn't surprised at the way she lay, since the weight of the motors and the heavy decompression chamber would have pulled her aft down.

"Can you see the chamber?" Jack asked, as he squinted his eyes from the sunlight pouring into the wheel house.

"No, nothing. She is sitting in a small V-shaped pile of coral and debris. We'll have to get down there and see," Ortiz said, excited and anxious to get below.

Juarez had called Señor Gomez the moment he was sure that they had discovered the boat, and suddenly the bridge was filled with people.

"Where is it? I want to see," Gomez demanded as he shoved Jack out of the way.

Several others muscled in close to take a peek, laughing and slapping each other on the back. The two topless women were standing tiptoed, leaning over the crowd of men trying to get a look. Perry was leaning against them copping a free feel. Jack caught his eye, "Nice boots ... *Partner*," Jack said in a malicious tone.

"What the fuck is that supposed to mean, asshole?" Perry answered back in the same tone.

"You were partners with Olsen, weren't you? You were there when Pointman was murdered in the cemetery. You killed him yourself or watched while Olsen killed him, then you took the boots off Point's feet ..."

Perry smashed a fist into Jack's face, knocking him down, "You don't know shit, Marsh. You need to learn to mind your own fucking business. Now, look at you. You're a fucking dead man walking, ya little fart knocker."

Gomez jerked Perry away from Jack as he was getting ready to unload a kick to his head.

"Stop this," Gomez yelled. "I need Marsh alive. I will let you kill him after he brings my money to me."

"Fucking whelp, I'll teach him," Perry said as he backed off.

Gomez snapped his fingers, "Capitán, let us begin the rescue of my ten million dollars," he said and called for everyone to follow him.

Jack and Ortiz made their way to the aft work deck, as the deck hand threw a buoy over the side marking the spot over the wreck. As Jack and Ortiz were putting their dive gear on, Gomez appeared with one of his guests.

"This is Manny; he will dive with you. His instructions are to watch and report everything you do, Jack, in case you try some funny business," Gomez said. "Ortiz, you are not to interfere with whatever Manny decides needs to be done. You take orders from him. *Preguntas*, questions?"

"No, Señor," Ortiz answered.

"Good, now go get my money."

Chapter 23

As the Zodiac rubber raft eased up to the buoy, Jack nabbed it and tied a painter line off to it. Ortiz cut the small 15 horsepower motor and set it up with the prop out of the water. Without a word, the three men put their fins on, slipped their masks down, and checked to make sure their breathing regulators were clear and functioning. After a few final adjustments of gear, the three gave thumbs up and rolled over backwards into the water.

Jack let air out of his B.C. to allow him to sink, flipped head-down, and started to kick for the bottom. The water was pristine, with almost unlimited visibility. Schools of fish were everywhere, all colors and shapes, some nosey, others scattering at the sight of three large predators invading their turf. Jack loved the ocean and spent hours with Tommy, whenever he could, diving on wrecks, spearfishing, and photographing sea life. Tommy and Jack would joke about who could drink the most seawater. So far, Tommy was the champ, and his trophy was a bad case of monkey-butt for a week. The sound of the exhaled air bubbles was almost musical, each giving off their own tone as they danced their way to the surface. The larger, dangerous species of fish swam out on the very fringe of visibility, where they watched for weakness or fear, then darted in for a quick kill.

At fifty feet, Jack flipped over to see where his partners were. Ortiz was off on his left a few meters back and gave Jack a thumbs up. Manny appeared to be struggling, still a good twenty feet above Jack. From Manny's movements, he could tell that Manny was not a good swimmer, and definitely not an experienced scuba diver. He was using his arms rather than kicking his feet to propel him, and was almost in a panic. Jack swam back to him and signaled for him to stop. With an experienced hand, he let air out of Manny's B.C. which would allow him to sink at a smooth rate, rather than the inflated vest trying to pull him back to the top. Jack held up his air gauge and pointed to it and compared his remaining air pressure with Manny's. Manny had already sucked up a third of his air, which meant he would have to surface sooner than Jack and Ortiz. Jack hand-signaled for Manny to control his breathing, then flipped over and headed for the bottom.

Schools of multicolored tropical fish had already taken up residence in the *Island Girl's* cabin and hull. A big brown Bahamas grouper peeked out at them as they approached, then pulled back deeper into the damaged bow. Jack set himself at neutral buoyancy, which allowed him to just float in place as he surveyed the wreck. It was amazing that the *Island Girl* was still as intact as she was after being beaten relentlessly by the storm. Ortiz signaled Jack to join him on the portside of the hull and pointed to a large piece of coral that had ripped a four-foot gap in the hull as it slipped down the incline and was the only thing keeping the wreck from sliding all the way into the depths. Both men swam back from the wreck to get a better view and saw that, from where the hull lay there was not another shelf below her, just sunless depths. The two swam close to the chamber to survey what they would need to do to free it from the moorings and get it to the top. During the storm, the chamber had broken free of the front two cables used to dog it down to the deck and now stuck out perpendicular to the hull, giving the overall appearance of a large L-shape, with the hull the vertical leg and the chamber the horizontal angle. Jack inspected the rear cables to see if they could get them off easily, but found them doubled and twisted. He then spent a few minutes checking the chamber's fittings and gauges. Tommy had purchased the chamber from the U.S. Navy which had scrapped it and replaced it with a newer version. Tommy felt with a few new gauges and rubber O-rings, it could be made serviceable. Jack's evaluation, now at almost ninety-five feet deep, was that it was a piece of crap.

Jack swam back to Ortiz and wrote on his chalkboard, 'hacksaw & air.' Ortiz gave him an affirmative nod and a thumbs up. With their survey complete, they headed for the surface. Jack looked around for Manny, but couldn't see him. Usually, it was easy to spot another diver by his air bubbles, but there were none in sight. Jack kicked for the bottom and searched the wreck to see if Manny had gotten himself tangled or caught on something. After a few minutes, he gave up and headed for the surface. When he broke the surface a few feet from the Zodiac, he spotted Manny sitting in the boat smiling sheepishly.

"I ran out of air," Manny said apologetically.

Jack pulled himself aboard and grabbed Manny by his B.C. "You dumb shit, you're no diver. What do you have, some stupid resort certification?" Jack said and shoved him away.

"This is my second dive. I told El Condor that I was an experienced diver so he would think I was brave and maybe get promoted someday …"

"And I guess your orders are to kill me if I do something wrong when we're down on the wreck?"

"Si, Señor Gomez told me to kill both of you if you tried anything that might prevent him from getting his money back. He told me he would give me five thousand dollars for each of you … if I needed to kill you.

"*Jeezus,* what a pig fuck." Jack said.

"I will tell you the truth. I was not going to kill you, no matter what. I will tell you, but please don't tell the Jefe, I have never killed anyone. Besides, I don't know enough to tell if you are doing something bad anyway."

Jack and Ortiz looked at each other and broke out laughing. "Lieutenant Ortiz, what we have here is a yes man, a sycophant wanna-be gangster, a Homey with no balls," Jack laughed.

"Señor Marsh, you do not understand. Señor Gomez is my auntie's husband's cousin. Without Señor Gomez's help, I would still be selling cigarettes on the streets of Havana. Please don't tell him that I failed as a diver. In return, I will tell the Señor how caring you are for his money, por favor, Señor," Manny pleaded.

Jack was disgusted and sympathetic at the same time. What an easy touch he was for a sob story. Here is this mutt who is supposed to kill him if he tries anything, and now he finds out that the kid is just a kid trying to get ahead, just like everybody else.

"Manny, don't worry, it's cool. I'll keep your secret. Enough people have already died for this money."

Chapter 24

After explaining to Gomez and the Capitán what they had found and what they were going to attempt to do, they went below, grabbed a sandwich, and went back to load the zodiac with what they would need on the next dive. Back over the dive site, Jack took four air tanks that he had attached lead weights to and lowered them over the side, feeding out line as they sank. At a hundred feet, the line went slack and he tied it off to the zodiac. They had agreed that Jack would do most of the work, since he was familiar with how the chamber had been dogged down. As he worked on the chamber, Ortiz would stand off clear of the wreck with a lifeline in hand with the other end tied to Jack. If the chamber, or the wreck, started to slip, then Ortiz was to pull Jack clear before being pulled down into the deep. Back on the yacht, they had confirmed that the depth at that particular spot was four hundred feet down and anything over two hundred feet would be fatal without the proper equipment.

Jack felt good about the plan and didn't think they would have any problems, but, with everything related to the ocean, something could always go wrong. You couldn't second guess her, nor outsmart her. You just had to be alert for anything. One mistake and she would take you down. Jack stood in the Zodiac taking one last look around the horizon for any sign of his rescuers. He was on his own. Another couple of hours, he could be with Billy, floating around the Bahamas Trench, but he wouldn't go down without a fight. If he was to die, then he was taking Gomez and that fat fuck Perry with him.

Jack and Ortiz exchanged looks, and flipped over the side, sinking quickly. Manny's job was to hang on to the line holding the air tanks as he descended, stopping whenever he felt too anxious or panicky, and not take any chances. When he felt Jack tug hard on the line, he was to clear the area.

The reef fish seemed to sense that something was about to happen as they flitted about watching the two divers head to the bottom. Nothing good ever came of something bigger than themselves swimming around, even the large predators had slunk away looking for a fight with something closer to their size. The sunlight had shifted from the earlier dive and now cast shadows at different angles, exposing debris and rubble not seen on the earlier dive. Ortiz swam over to a mound of old coral encrusted car tires that must have been dumped years ago, perhaps to build up the reef over time.

Away from the tires was a sandy slope that had hundreds of expended brass 20mm shell casings which reflected the light like gold bars. Back the other way, was an aircraft frame eaten away by the salt water, its canopy shone like a mirror, reflecting off a kaleidoscope of dazzling colors.

Near the wreck, Jack realized that the coral rubble was a mix of dead coral, pieces of shrapnel from exploded rocket casings, and dozens of unexploded rockets. Jack's knowledge of rockets was nonexistent except for what he had seen on the Military Channel. But his guess was that these babies were lethal, no matter for what their usage was intended, surface to surface, air to air, didn't matter from where he floated. One false move and he was fucked.

Ortiz swam over and held up his marker board with a big question mark on it. Jack shrugged and signaled back with an ok. Jack tied the life line to his belt and handed the coiled line to Ortiz, gave him thumbs up, and swam to the wreck. The weighted air tanks sat on the shelf next to the wreck, swaying gently. Jack untied one and pulled it to his chest as he swam to the chamber. At the chamber, he snapped one end of an air hose to a fitting and gave it a tug to make sure it was seated. The other end of the hose was already attached to the tank, so Jack just needed to turn the nozzle to feed air into the chamber from the tank. Jack opened the nozzle slowly and could feel the tank kick a little from releasing pressure. A hissing noise could be heard as the air entered the chamber. When the hissing stopped, Jack disconnected the hose and let it sink. He repeated the process with the second air tank. The chamber groaned as it became buoyant and tried to rise.

The next step was going to be the dangerous one. Jack swam down to the *Island Girl's* deck, checked the port side cables holding that end of the chamber in place, and then the starboard side cables. He sucked in air and started sawing with the hacksaw. It took less than a minute to cut through the starboard cables. The chamber's steel plates screamed as they contorted and rolled to port where the cable still held the chamber in place, as the freed end swung up shifting the weight of the wreck. The hull groaned and popped as Jack felt the boat sliding. He kicked his fins and jetted backwards clear of the wreck. A cloud of coral dust hid the wreck as she slid, screaming and groaning from the pain of scrapes and gouges to her hull, finally coming to a stop with half her hull hanging over the precipice. The *Island Girl* appeared to totter back and forth before it settled back into the rubble.

The stakes had just gone up exponentially as Jack weighed the odds of his cutting the last strands of cable before she slid over the side. He wanted to make sure he wasn't going to go down with her and watched from a few meters back from the chamber. After thinking about the best way to finish this up, Jack scribbled on his marker board and held it up for Ortiz to read, 'U attach the 3rd air tank & fill on my signal = 2 taps. I will cut as u fill.'

Ortiz gave a thumbs up and retrieved an air tank from the rubble shelf and took his position at the end of the tank. Jack looked up, searching for Manny, but there was no sign of him. Jack smiled as he swam back to the chamber. The wreck groaned as Jack knelt on the deck, sticking his head under the chamber to get a look at the cables. Satisfied that he had a clear view of the cables, he put the hacksaw blade on the closest one and started sawing. Within seconds, the cable snapped, causing the chamber to shift, catching Jack's hand between the deck and the steel plate. The pain wasn't bad, but he was trapped. He couldn't free his hand. He hit the chamber two sharp raps and could feel the weight lifting off his hand as Ortiz opened the valve and released air into the chamber. The chamber shifted again as it got lighter, which took weight off the wreck, and it began to slide. Jack's heart was pounding as he felt everything shifting below him. His hand was trapped and the boat was teetering on the lip of the shelf. Ortiz emptied the tank as quickly as the air would flow. The chamber was light and pulling, fighting desperately to shoot to the surface. It pulled against the last cable as it tugged. The *Island Girl* slipped over the lip and was trying to break free of the chamber, so it could plunge down into the depths. The wreck was winning as it swept over the side and started its dive. Jack was desperate as he was being dragged to his death. He put the hacksaw blade against the stretched wire cable and started sawing as he plunged with the boat. Suddenly, there was a loud *POP* and the chamber rocketed to the surface. Jack was free and he kicked away from the *Island Girl* as she picked up speed. Jack's depth gauge had him at 150 feet. He was sucking air fast from the fear and the exertion, but still took time to watch the chamber rocket to the surface. It was like a watery space shuttle lifting off, never seen before.

Suddenly, it disappeared as it broke free of the water and went airborne before splashing down ten meters from where it left the water.

Jack swam back to the shelf and retrieved the fourth air tank, knowing he would need it after going so deep. He would have to make several ascent stops on his way up so he didn't get the bends. Ortiz was already on the surface, and Manny, at the helm of the zodiac, was circling around to pick him up. Jack took one last look around at the rubble field where the *Island Girl* had been, then gave a couple of strong kicks that propelled him upwards. He was worried about what fate awaited him once he was back on board the *Malagueña* as he heard a deep rumbling of sound carried by the water. He stopped and looked off in the distance, but couldn't see anything. The Doppler waves of sound told him it was a motor and it was moving towards him. Jack's spirits lifted immediately as he realized that this could be the cavalry coming to rescue him. He was so excited that he almost passed his forty-five-foot ascent pause. It would be a fifteen-minute wait as his body burned off the carbon dioxide build-up, then he would have to stop for five minutes at thirty feet before surfacing.

Chapter 25

Topside, the U.S. Coast Guard Frigate *Mobile* was up on plane, running across the water at thirty-three knots. Her forward gun mount had fired a round across the bow of the *Malagueña* as she had weighed anchor and was trying to make a run south for Cuban waters. The Skipper aboard the *Mobile* had his radio operator in contact with the *Malagueña's* bridge, telling her to cut her engines and stand by to be boarded. Alongside the Skipper were Captain Price and Lt. Mathers, both looking anxious and concerned that they might be too late to save Jack Marsh. The news that Marsh had contacted Coco Duvalier had not reached them until after seven this morning. After trying to cut through several layers of command and control, the two Florida lawmen were successful in getting the Coast Guard on board and away from their base in Key West. It had been a flat-out sprint from the time they cleared Key West Harbor's outer markers until they had picked up the *Malagueña* on radar. The news that Billy Short had been killed tore Lt. Mathers up, and that Sheriff Perry was aboard and watched it, was maddening.

The bridge of the *Malagueña* was splattered with Capitán Juarez's blood. His lifeless body lay in a heap by the chart table where Gomez had left it. When Juarez had refused Gomez's order to make a run for Cuban waters, but instead wanted to comply with the Coast Guard's orders to stop engines, Gomez smashed his head into the metal bulkhead, killing him instantly. Gomez was now at the wheel and had the engines redlined, unconsciously rocking his body back and forth trying to get more speed out of her by sheer force of will. He shouted orders to start firing on the Navy ship, hoping that it would slow them down long enough for him to make it into

Cuban waters. Several of his men came up on deck with M16 rifles and started firing at the oncoming vessel. Sheriff Perry went below, thinking fast how he could turn this to his favor. He checked the load on his Sig and headed for the bridge.

Captain McBride, aboard the *Mobile,* realized they were under fire when the bridge windscreen cracked and a small bullet hole appeared.

"What the hell? They're shooting at us," he said, shocked that someone would have the audacity to shoot at the U.S. Coast Guard. "Chief, tell Clancy to sweep the bridge with the twenty mike-mike."

"Aye, aye, Sir," came the reply.

The bridge of the *Malagueña* disintegrated in splinters of metal and plastic as the 20mm rounds chewed up everything they hit. Three of the men who had been firing from the bridge wing lay dead in pools of blood and gore. Gomez was at the wheel, turning in zigzag sweeps across the water, kicking up a rooster-tail of spray, but the 20mm rounds kept chewing the cabin up. Perry crawled onto the bridge, keeping low as he snuck up behind Gomez, pointed the muzzle of his pistol at the Condor's spine, and fired three rounds. Gomez stiffened for a moment and collapsed, dead. Perry stood and cut the throttles back to neutral and hit the power button, shutting everything down. The four remaining thugs ran to the bridge, saw their master dead, and dropped their weapons.

Perry got on the radio. "This is Sheriff Perry, I have successfully taken over the boat, it is safe to come alongside, I repeat …"

"Now, what game is he playing?" Mathers said to Price.

The boarding party of armed sailors took little time securing the *Malagueña*, cuffing the gunmen and the women with zip lock strips. Captain Price and Lt. Mathers had cuffed Perry with little trouble. The fat man was so surprised that he was being treated as a criminal that he began kicking and screaming like a wild man.

"Get these off me right now, Mathers. How dare you? I'll have your ass for this," Perry said in his best self-righteous voice. "I have, you know I've been working undercover, and if it weren't for me, Gomez would have gotten away from you."

"Shut up, Perry," Price said as he hustled Perry down the ladder and into the Coast Guard's whale boat.

Mathers had searched below decks trying to find Marsh, with no luck. In the crew's quarters, he found an old man hiding in his bunk and he motioned with his pistol for the man to come out.

"I am an honest man, Señor. Please do not shoot me. I have a fat wife and many children in Miami who need their Papa …"

"Shut up old man, I'm not going to shoot you. Have you seen a gringo named Jack Marsh?"

"Si."

"Well?' Mathers said.

"Jack, Teniente Ortiz, and Manny went to get the money."

"Where did they go?" Mathers was losing patience with the man.

The old man pointed his index finger down in answer.

"Down? Down where?"

"Down to the bottom of the sea, Señor. Where else?"

Mathers shook his head and prodded the old man topside. The boarding party had secured the boat and was preparing it for towing back to their Key West base. Price and Mathers were standing on the bridge when a bos'n's mate pointed off to the horizon, where a red signal flare was floating down.

"What the hell …" the boson said, as he focused his binoculars.

"Here give me those," Mathers said, and snatched them from the man. He put them to his eyes, adjusted the focus, and let out a loud laugh. "I'll be damned," he said as he saw a rubber Zodiac with two men in it with a long line pulling a metal cylinder behind it. And there was Jack Marsh, sitting astride the cylinder, waving like a damn cowboy riding a rodeo bull.

Chapter 26

Jack had been given a pair of crew dungarees and had a steaming cup of coffee in his hands as he told Captain Price and Lt. Mathers his story from beginning to end. A third man was introduced to Jack as representing the *Agency*, but no name was offered. The man had a small satellite transmitter that he placed in front of Jack, adjusting it every now and then as he spoke low into a chin microphone. Several times the man had Jack repeat the parts regarding the killing of Colonel Carson at Santa Cruz Del Norte and the circumstances leading up to his being shot and what the Spec Op team did after the shooting.

"Did the First Sergeant Otis give you any indication that he was aborting his mission or otherwise not carrying out Colonel Carson's orders?"

Jack thought for a moment then answered, "Mister, that Sergeant was the only professional out there that night. If Colonel Carson was *your* man, then it's no wonder things are as fucked up as they are …"

"Now, hold it right there," a voice boomed from the speaker. "You just watch your mouth, Marsh, or you'll be pounding sand down at Gitmo … *insubordinate little shit,*" the voice trailed off.

Jack cracked up laughing, "Gitmo! "You fucking clowns, you're going to put me in Gitmo? You threaten me like that I'll be on CNN, FOX, Judge Judy, and every other TV station before the sun goes down …" Jack was just so frustrated he wanted to reach out and hit someone. "This interview is over, Mr. Agency Ass Hat," he said and poured his coffee over the speaker.

"What the fuck, Marsh!" the agent across from Jack snapped, as he grabbed the apparatus and shook coffee off of it. "You're fucking out of control, man. We're just trying to figure out what happened that night. The team is missing and we don't know if they are dead, captured, or what."

"My money's on the First Sergeant being alive and on the run, and if you guys had any balls you would've gotten them out by now," Jack barked right back at the man.

Captain Price put a hand on Jack's shoulder, "Cool down, Marsh. Nobody's sending you anywhere, you're under my protection. Tell these guys what you know, then we'll get back to what you were saying about Perry.

An hour later, the agency man packed up his gear. At the door, Jack called out to him, "What about follow up? What should I say if anyone ever asks?" Jack was surprised that he wasn't asked to swear an oath of silence or allegiance to *The Agency*, or if he did ever breathe a word of what he knew, would he be "*taken out with extreme prejudice?*"

"Loose ends, I hate them," Jack mumbled.

The agent turned and looked at Jack, pointed an imaginary finger-pistol at him and mouthed, *BANG*, then was out the door.

"Swell! Now I'll go through life always wondering if that was a yes or no."

"Let it go, Jack. You'll never see or hear from them again. They just needed to cover their asses in case their little operation is ever discovered," Price said with a shrug. "Now let's get back to Sheriff Perry. Run through what you know before we bring him in here."

Jack filled his coffee cup from the pot and began, "Well, the cowboy boots are the key. Pointman was wearing them the day he came in to see me at the Sand Bar. He told me that he had taken them off of the dead man that the killers threw out of the car before they sped away. Later, when I went to identify Pointman at the morgue, he wasn't wearing the boots and when I asked about his personal belongings Sgt. Short said that he didn't have any. I asked about the boots and was told that he was brought in wearing the pair of underwear that I had given him earlier that day and nothing else. Sgt. Short had a copy of the investigating officer's report right there in his hands. The next time I saw the boots was aboard the *Malagueña* as Sheriff Perry was wiping Sgt. Short's blood off of them on the back of his trousers after Short's blood had splattered them. The next time I saw them was this morning on the bridge of the *Malagueña* when I accused Perry of being partners with Agent Olsen and that he or Olsen killed Pointman in the cemetery."

"What happened then?" Lt. Mathers asked.

"He called me a little fart knocker and smashed me in the face. The same slang name that Pointman quoted as having heard the killer say the night the man was murdered at the deserted Navy facility. Pointman said he laughed when he heard that expression, since he hadn't heard it since he was a kid in Waco."

Captain Price flipped his notebook closed and looked at Lt. Mathers. "I think we have enough to nail his ass. Let's get him in here and squeeze him." Captain Price turned to Jack, "Marsh, we've been holding Perry separate from the others, so he doesn't know that you're here on board. As far as he knows you're on the bottom, a victim of Gomez's orders to kill you once the chamber was retrieved. I want you to wait on the bridge until I call you down, ok?"

Jack was standing alongside the Captain on the bridge as the frigate cut through the water at twenty-five knots, heading for Key West.

"I don't want to alarm you, Mr. Marsh, but it's been reported that the fish around that reef are highly radioactive from all the munitions on the bottom and if you were to eat one you would probably die. Some old timers say that if you even get in those waters, you'll probably glow in the dark," the Captain said with a sly grin on his face.

Jack looked around the bridge and saw the other crew members smiling, "You damned swabbies are always trying to scare us poor old jarheads. Well it's payback time," Jack said as he pulled a 20mm shell made from depleted uranium out of his dungaree cargo pocket — he had grabbed it from the bottom to keep as a souvenir of his adventure — and placed it on the chart table with a magician's flourish.

"If I'm going to glow, we're all going to glow."

Everyone on the bridge jumped back in mock horror and fear. A chorus of, "No, no, not the depleted uranium trick," and "Arg, we're all going to die ..." "Abandon ship ..."

Everyone was still laughing when Jack was called back down to the small cabin being used for debriefing. Sheriff Perry's back was to Jack as he entered the cabin. Perry heard the hatchway door close behind him and turned to see who had joined them. When he saw Jack, he sprang up and grabbed him by the throat. "This is the little fart knocker who killed Sgt. Short, and all the others. Ya fucking murderer," he screamed as he tightened his chokehold.

The sudden attack caught Jack by surprise and he fell back against the door, trying to break Perry's hold. Perry's face was livid with rage. His eyes were crazed, and spit was flying from his flabby jowls as he dug his fat stubby fingers into Jack's neck. "I'll kill you, Marsh, you fucking troublemaker. Olsen was right, you need killing ..." Perry screamed, and then realized what he had said and pushed Jack away from him, spinning around to confront his inquisitors.

"You dumb fucking people call yourselves law enforcement officers, when you ain't shit. The only way to beat criminals at their own game is to kill 'em ... kill 'em all. All the wishy-washy rules will get you killed. That fucking wino never should have been allowed to walk the city streets. He was nothing. He tried to steal all that money for what? Then you got Olsen. The man was corrupt, on the take, sold his soul to El Condor, and died begging for mercy. At least I knew what I was doing with Gomez. Take as much as I could grab from the lowlife sumbitch, then kill him ... yeah, that's right. I killed Gomez and Olsen, the nigger, and the wino, and that shit who tried to double-cross me and tried to keep the money for himself. I wanted that money just as bad as Gomez did. Then fucking Marsh comes along and sticks his punk nose in my business ..."

Perry was working his way around the table toward Mathers as he spoke, hunched forward like a demonic wrestler, fingers flexing and grasping, wheezing as he spoke, a physical threat to everyone in the room. Price was going for his pistol as Jack lunged for Perry, jumping on his back, wrapping his arms around the big head and neck. Perry spun around in a whir of motion trying to throw Jack off his back, finally crashing into the bulkhead, breaking Jack's hold. Perry came around with a mighty kick that caught Jack in the head, knocking him unconscious.

Chapter 27

Jack was sitting on his stool at the end of the bar sipping coffee watching Lamont set up for the day's business as Coco was busy running numbers on her calculator, mumbling to herself. It was going to be another hot day in paradise, according to the Keynoter News that Jack had spread out on the bar. The town was still all a-twitter about Sheriff Perry being charged with multiple murders and how Jack Marsh — a local business owner — had played a key role in his apprehension. Lt. Mathers made sure that Sgt. Short was hailed as the real hero for bringing down the El Condor drug cartel, and shutting down the huge money laundering pipeline operation Gomez had been running through the Keys. Sgt. Short, working under cover, had exposed the ring and dealt it a death blow out on the high seas in a gun battle that resulted in Gomez and four of his men being killed. Details were still sketchy, but the Keynoter was assured all would come out in Sheriff Perry's trial, scheduled in two months' time.

Coco stopped her work for a moment and looked at Jack, "Tell me again how we're going to pay for all these repairs and new equipment that I've been buying to replace all the things the police broke or ruined."

Jack took a sip of his coffee and looked at Coco. "Easy. One thing I've learned over the last month is that everyone can be bought. What you do is, when you get the final bill from a supplier, you go visit him and offer cash in payment, plus fifteen percent under the table. He'll jump at the cash, pocket the fifteen percent, and carry the original invoice as a collectable which increases the value of his business when he goes for a loan."

"And then?" Coco asked chewing on the end of her pencil.

"And then, by doing what I just outlined, we work off the bundle of cash we have that doesn't exist," Jack said with a big smile.

"I think I'll let you do the visiting and I'll just mind the store, if you don't mind," Coco said trying to keep at arm's length what her boss was proposing.

"No problem, Ms. Duvalier. Leave the strategic thinking to me, and you tend to the operational issues. Now pour me a little more coffee, woman," Jack said, holding his empty cup out, looking back down at his newspaper.

"Mr. Marsh, last time I checked, I was the brains of this operation, strategic or otherwise, so fetch your own damn coffee," she said and hustled off.

Jack chuckled to himself and continued his search for any news of the Special Operations team that they had dropped off in Cuba. Ever since the one interview aboard the Coast Guard frigate, Jack hadn't heard a word from any agency or person. Jack still felt that if anyone could survive and evade capture in Cuba it would be First Sergeant Otis and his team. Even if they had missed their rendezvous and pick-up with the submarine, Jack felt that they would head for the Guantanamo base at the east end of the island and make it out that way. He hoped this was the case, although he would never know.

Even Don Cona and Junior had disappeared. Junior was still in the hospital with a serious infection in his intestines when Tommy and little Mikey had been released. Then one morning he was gone. Every morning Jack expected to see the old man hobble in on Junior's arm and order his espresso and shot of whiskey, but they never did.

Tommy was lost without the *Island Girl*, but he had found a good deal on a sixty-eight footer rigged as a dive and salvage boat up in the boat yard in Marathon. The man who owned it had just completed an overhaul on the engines and mechanical parts. He had put in all new electronics the month before, then keeled over and died from a heart attack while inspecting it. His wife wanted to dump it fast and move back up to the mainland, so would be ready to deal when Tommy and Jack could make it up to see it. Neither Jack or Tommy were worried about getting a new boat financed since the insurance claim on the *Island Girl* was working its way through the bureaucracy and would be settled soon. No mention of the Cuban Navy shooting and sinking them was made to the insurance company because of some dumb 'Act of War' clause that would have nixed the payout.

Tommy still had his bundle of cash hidden away and was feeding off it to replace his old income from his black-market sales with Miguel Santos out in the Straits every week. The cash in the bundle would actually keep him in money for a long time and he wasn't hurting for anything. He was still posing as little Mike's father and had enrolled him in a private Christian school across town. Mike was still very quiet, but was coming along well and seemed to grow closer to Tommy and Mimi every day. Mike never spoke of his father and what happened out in the storm. His young mind was protecting itself and wasn't ready to deal with it. Mimi had rented a nice place over on one of the canals and furnished it with all new furniture while they looked for a new place of their own, maybe out on Cudjo Key.

A week ago when Jack had felt that things were cooling down with the law and with any bad guys who might still be lingering in the weeds watching him, Jack met Tommy at the Dive Hut and they closed and locked the doors after rolling the oil drum inside. Satisfied that no one could peek in or see what they were doing, they popped open the fifty-five-gallon drum and began to count the two bags of cash they had stashed out of the ten million. After two counts, they sat back with big shit-eating grins. The final count was two million one hundred sixty-eight thousand, four hundred ... even.

"Let's count it again, just for fun," Tommy said.

"Ok," Jack answered.

—

The strong air conditioning unit was blowing frosty air out of the vents into the Sand Bar, keeping it cool as the water vapor units cooled the outside seating area. Tourists from the ship were already working the shops up and down Duval while the less brave sucked up ice cold beer and burger baskets inside the Sand Bar. Arturo was on his perch, preening, keeping a sharp eye out for someone to insult. The new girl, Barbie, was everything and more, that Coco said she was. The male customers couldn't get their drinks down fast enough so they could order again from the babe in the halter. Jack knew right away that he would have to have a talk with Lamont about Barbie. Lamont was in love, no doubt about it, and he was headed for the heartbreak hotel if he thought he was going to sweep Barbie off her feet. It wasn't in the cards.

Jack suddenly had a deep feeling of satisfaction about his life here in the Keys and how he had never felt happier. He strolled across the street and turned, looking at his place, The Sand Bar. 'Yeah, I could stay here forever …'

"Hey, Jacky, you need a cab?" The guy called out as the old cab pulled to the curb.

"Nah, just standing around enjoying the day. How ya doing?" Jack called back.

"You know how it is, good days, bad days, come see, come saw, it all works out."

"Don't I know it, Bro," Jack answered with a wave.

XXXX

Made in the USA
San Bernardino, CA
02 April 2017